WITNESS

TO WAR

The Sequel to *Witness to Revolution: Growing Up in Williamsburg During the American Revolution*

MICHAEL & JENNIFER CECERE

HERITAGE BOOKS
2024

HERITAGE BOOKS
AN IMPRINT OF HERITAGE BOOKS, INC.

Books, CDs, and more—Worldwide

For our listing of thousands of titles see our website
at
www.HeritageBooks.com

Published 2024 by
HERITAGE BOOKS, INC.
Publishing Division
5810 Ruatan Street
Berwyn Heights, MD 20740

Cover art: Painting *Uphill Struggle* by Bryant White

Page 59 with caption "College Company":
Painting *Boys Company of Williamsburg* by Bryant White

International Standard Book Number
Paperbound: 978-0-7884-2787-9

Table of Contents

Chapter 1	Something Has Changed	Winter 1777	1
Chapter 2	No One Seems to Care Anymore	1778	19
Chapter 3	Militia Service	1778-79	31
Chapter 4	The College Company Marches	1779	51
Chapter 5	James Graduates	1779	73
Chapter 6	We Must Endure This Separation	1779	93
Chapter 7	Home for Christmas	1779	107
Chapter 8	John Joins the Continentals	1780	125
Chapter 9	Goodbye	1780	141
Chapter 10	Battle of Waxhaws	May 1780	151
Chapter 11	The Army Reforms in Hillsborough	June 1780	171

Chapter 12	What News of John? Summer 1780	187
Chapter 13	Battle of Camden August 1780	211
Chapter 14	Back to Hillsborough Fall 1780	225
Chapter 15	Virginia Is Alarmed Fall 1780	247

Acknowledgements

This book, like the first one, could not have been written without collaboration with my daughter, Jennifer. Somehow, she managed to squeeze time to work on the book in Japan out of the time she spent caring for her newborn child (my first grandchild). Working thirteen time zones apart from each other was challenging enough, but to add the demands of a baby into the mix required a herculean effort on her part to complete the book. I am very grateful, Jen, for your time and help, without which neither of these books could have happened.

My friends at Colonial Williamsburg also deserve recognition for their steadfast dedication to telling America's past in an authentic manner. There is no better place in the world to inspire folks about the American Revolution than Colonial Williamsburg, and I appreciate all that the foundation and its wonderful people do. Thanks also go to the very talented artist, Bryant White, who allowed us to use two of his paintings—one of which is the cover—for the book. The fine folks at Heritage Books were also very helpful, especially Debbie Riley who helped edit the book.

About the Authors

Michael Cecere is a retired History teacher who resides in Williamsburg, Virginia with his wife, Susan. Originally from Maine, he taught high school and college level American History for thirty years in Virginia. The author of over twenty books and numerous articles on the American Revolution and Revolutionary War, he continues to research and write in retirement.

When he is not writing, Mr. Cecere volunteers and works at Colonial Williamsburg, sometimes as a tobacco farmer, other times as a soldier or a colonial dancer. He also participates in Revolutionary War reenactments throughout the east coast and lectures at historic sites and historical societies.

Jennifer Cecere Miyazaki is a passionate writer like her father, but until now, has kept her writing mostly to herself. She grew up in Virginia but has spent the majority of her post-university life in Tokyo, Japan, where she now resides with her husband, their dog, and newborn daughter. In addition to her love of writing, she enjoys teaching—particularly children—and has spent the past decade inspiring young learners to follow their dreams.

When she is not writing or teaching, she can be found having long-distance conversations with her family, out in nature with her family, or on the couch with a book in hand.

Introduction

This is the second of three books that we hope will enlighten readers about the American Revolution and Revolutionary War. Written as historical fiction about the lives of three young people growing up in Williamsburg, Virginia during the Revolution, great effort has been made to present their stories as historically accurate as possible.

Our hope is that readers will develop a stronger understanding and appreciation of the American Revolution and the struggle and sacrifice it took to secure our independence as a nation.

The first book, *Witness to Revolution*, spanned the years 1771 through 1777 and explored critical events that led to America's declaration of independence. The outbreak of war in 1775 and the events that followed impacted every Virginian and were witnessed by brothers James and John Southall, and their friend Rebecca Anderson—three children growing up in Williamsburg.

In this book, *Witness to War*, James, John, and Rebecca are teenagers living in a new nation that is three years into its war for independence. The war is distant, happening mostly in the North, but seems to be getting closer with each passing season, especially for James and John, who turn sixteen—the age of compulsory militia service—in December of 1778 and 1779 respectively. James ends up serving in the militia, and John in the Continental army—each participating in the war just as Rebecca feared. The war touches Rebecca and her family as well when they leave Williamsburg in 1780 and relocate to Virginia's new capital, Richmond. The impact the war has on these three friends and their families is thus the focus of this book.

Chapter One

Something Has Changed

Winter 1777

Thirteen-year-old Rebecca Anderson leaned against a tree overlooking her favorite brook behind Mr. Dixon's print shop in Williamsburg, Virginia. She shivered in the cold November air and let out a sigh. One could well argue that she should be in high spirits, seeing as just a few days earlier she had attended her first ball at the Capitol. It was in celebration of the American victory over the British at Saratoga, New York. An entire British army of several thousand had surrendered in October and the sting of losing Philadelphia to the British in late September was briefly soothed by the good news of Saratoga. But Rebecca's thoughts lingered not on celebration and dancing, but on war.

Perhaps this will finally convince them to leave us alone, Rebecca thought as she waited for her two friends to join her. *Please let it be so for James's and John's sake; three years of war is long enough.*

James and John Southall were Rebecca's dearest friends. Born and raised in Williamsburg, the three had weathered the past years' struggle for American independence together. Though as children, they were largely shielded from the brunt of it all. War was something they heard a lot about, but they themselves were kept far from it. With each passing day, however, that distance felt shorter and shorter, as the boys fast approached the age of military service—sixteen. James was the oldest, just a few weeks away from fifteen, and his brother John was just a year behind. Rebecca feared that soon her friends would be snatched away from her.

Rebecca had met the two brothers when her family moved into widow Wetherburn's tavern in Williamsburg six years earlier, in 1771. Wetherburn's had become available to rent that year because its former tenant, James Southall, the boys' father, had purchased the Raleigh Tavern across the street.

Rebecca smiled as she remembered their first meeting. She had been seated on the porch of her family's new tavern when eight-year-old James approached from across the street. Her first instinct had been to dash inside, but she worried that would appear rude, so she stood and prepared to meet him instead.

James had bowed formally as he introduced himself and Rebecca replied with a curtsey. Shortly after, John had burst upon the scene and introduced himself—far less formally.

He'd tried to scare me with stories of ghosts, Rebecca chuckled as she remembered John's claim that her new home was haunted. *And his dancing*, she thought, *how awful. I wanted nothing to do with him after our first dance lesson together!*

It was true. Their first dance *was* a disaster and John had little interest in dancing, but it was something his mother insisted every respectable Virginian should do well. And so, John had no choice. He grudgingly continued with his lessons over the years and his performance at the recent ball was proof of his progress.

What a night, Rebecca thought, recalling the grandeur of her first ball. *It was perfect.*

James and John arrived as Rebecca reminisced. "There you are, Becca," announced John, "you blended into the tree so well that we almost didn't see you."

Rebecca turned to face them and curtsied as both boys half bowed, not out of disrespect, but familiarity. Like Rebecca, they each thought of her as their best friend, and they had long ago ceased with the rigid formality of 18th century colonial society when they were together.

"Sorry to keep you waiting," James said. "Father was scolding John for—"

"Becca doesn't seem to mind," John interrupted. "Look at her. I've never seen her smile so wide."

Rebecca laughed. "Yes, well. Perhaps it froze that way. Seeing as I have been out here in the cold for quite a while. Waiting."

John reddened and mumbled an apology, but Rebecca waved it off. "I don't mind. It's been nice. I was thinking about the ball. How beautiful everything was."

"It was rather nice," agreed John. "But I for one am glad it is over and would be content to never attend another."

James rolled his eyes. "That's because you dance like a donkey."

Rebecca laughed again. "I thought you both danced excellently. A marked improvement from our first dance lesson together."

Both brothers smiled at that.

"That is kind of you to say, Becca," said James. "It was a lovely evening. And you were an absolute sensation."

Rebecca looked down at her feet to hide her scarlet cheeks. "Well, you two were dashing yourselves."

There was an awkward pause for a moment. Rebecca could feel James's eyes on her and wished he'd look away. At least until she felt less flushed. She pushed herself off the tree trunk and turned to walk, her back to the boys. *We need to talk about something other than the dance*, she thought. "Do you return to school tomorrow, James?"

The boys fell into step behind her. "I do," replied James, "after church. I have several more weeks of study before Christmas."

James was in his fourth year at William & Mary. He had spent his first two years at the grammar school and his most recent two at the college. The students had all lost a year of instruction in 1775-76 when the war broke out, but James hoped to complete his studies in another year and a half.

"It should be a fine Christmas this year," predicted John, "now that we've turned the tables on old King George."

"Perhaps," replied James. "But don't forget, they still have Philadelphia and New York."

"Not for long," John shot back. "The papers say we've blocked the river and the British navy can't reach Philadelphia. So General Howe and his redcoats will have to leave, else they'll starve there."

John's optimistic prediction would prove to be only partially correct. General Washington's troops did indeed obstruct the Delaware River for over two months after the British captured Philadelphia in September, and this *did* prevent the British navy from supplying General Howe's army in the city. The fort defending the American river obstructions fell to the British, however, on the very day Williamsburg celebrated the victory at Saratoga with a ball. This meant the British Army in Philadelphia now had a secure naval supply line which allowed them to remain comfortably in Philadelphia for as long as they wished.

Within a month, it would be the *American* army under General Washington who would struggle to feed itself in their winter encampment at Valley Forge, twenty-five miles outside of Philadelphia.

But the three friends were, of course, not aware of these developments and hoped that this Christmas would be the last Christmas of war.

The afternoon passed quickly with much laughter and before they knew it, it was time to leave. John and Rebecca agreed to return to the brook the next day after church, but James couldn't join them because he had to return to school after the service.

On the walk back home, Rebecca's thoughts turned once more to the ball. She had tried to ignore it, but something *had* changed that night between her and the boys. She still could not quite put her finger on it, but that same electric tension she felt at the ball had appeared this morning when James complimented her. Never before had his gaze made her feel so flustered. In fact, previously she had paid little attention to where James decided to hone his attention. But now, strangely, she both wanted his attention *and* wished he'd place it elsewhere. Which was, of course, impossible.

Rebecca had been sought after by many of the young gentlemen at the ball, and at first, she'd thought James's determination to dance with her was simply due to wanting to protect her. Perhaps he could tell how tired she was of laughing at bad jokes and smiling awkwardly at compliments from boys who, not so long ago, had teased her for her clumsiness and red hair. But there was something about the way James looked at her that night. She did not know what it was, but it made her heartbeat quicken. Something *was* different.

Rebecca's friendship with James was not the only thing that seemed different after the dance. As the Southalls and Andersons walked together up Duke of Gloucester Street to attend church, teenage boy after teenage boy went out of their way to greet Rebecca, something that had never occurred before.

"Good day, Miss Anderson," shouted 15-year-old Adam Craig as Rebecca passed the Golden Ball—his home and his father's goldsmith shop. "Your hat is splendid."

Rebecca paused, faced her admirer, and curtsied, her cheeks flush with embarrassment. "Why thank you Mr. Craig, you are kind to say so."

Rebecca's parents, who were walking just ahead of her, shared a smile. To them, their daughter had always been a vision of beauty. Now—after Rebecca's stunning display at the ball—it appeared that all the young gentlemen of Williamsburg were of the same opinion.

Two similar encounters occurred further along the walk to the church, and the attention continued even after the service, with several young suitors gathered around Rebecca in the churchyard.

"You were wonderful at the ball, Miss Anderson," gushed 15-year-old John Carter.

"Indeed you were," agreed 14-year-old Richard Charlton.

Rebecca did her best to hide her discomfort. She wanted to find James before he left for school, but it would be rude to ignore her new admirers.

She curtsied to both, one at a time. "It was indeed a grand evening," she replied, a smile fixed on her face but her eyes scanning just above the boys' heads. "Everyone looked so elegant."

James and John stood off to the side, hidden amongst the small crowd. They watched with a mixture of amusement and concern as the young gentlemen—no, *intruders*—fawned over their friend.

Finally, Rebecca spotted James, just as he turned away to walk to the college. She moved forward to step past the boys, bowing her head in apology. "It was wonderful talking with you but I really must—"

"Could I walk you home, Miss Anderson?" Richard Charlton blurted out, his arm blocking her exit.

James had exited the churchyard and was now in the street, heading for the school. "Well I—"

Thankfully, Rebecca did not need to finish her sentence. Her father had come to her rescue, stepping forward and offering his arm. "Come my dear, we must be off."

She took his arm gratefully and the boys parted to let them pass. After they exited the churchyard, Rebecca stopped and turned to her father. "Excuse me, Father, but I must say goodbye to James." She dashed up the street and called out, "James, James!" to get his attention.

James turned and smiled as he watched her run to him. He was touched she had come to say goodbye.

"I just wanted to wish you well for the remainder of your term," she said between breaths.

James chuckled. "Thank you, Becca. But you didn't have to run to tell me that."

"I was afraid you'd leave before I could see you," she panted. She took a deep breath and regained her composure. "I miss you every time you go back."

And there it was again, that look. *Tenderness*, thought Rebecca. *It is like how Father sometimes looks at Mother.*

James lowered his head, but he could not hide the red of his cheeks. "I miss you too, Becca," he said quietly. "But it's just for a few more weeks. We'll be together at the brook again before Christmas."

Rebecca studied him carefully. She could not see his eyes now for he refused to meet her gaze, but she was certain of what she had seen. "Well," she said with a smile, "until then, let *this* keep me in your thoughts as you are always in mine." She leaned in close and kissed him on his cheek.

James stood stunned as Rebecca whirled around and scampered back to her waiting parents. She had never done anything like that before, and James did not know what to make of it. Even Rebecca, who had been the one to act, was stunned. What had come over her?

"Well, well, well," whispered John to himself, having seen the whole thing from afar. *We'll certainly have something to talk about at the brook*, he thought.

When Rebecca arrived at the brook later that afternoon, John met her with a sly smile. "Rebecca," he said loudly. "How was church?"

There was a gleam in John's eye and he seemed even more cocky than usual. Rebecca arched her brows at him. "What do you mean?"

"Oh, you know. Just curious if anything interesting happened. After the service. Anything I might have missed."

"Oh, well Richard Charlton asked to walk me home, if that's what you mean." Rebeca settled herself along the edge of the brook, eyes straight ahead on the water. "Thankfully my father intervened."

"Ah, yes. I saw that." John sat down beside her. "But I was talking about what happened after you left church." He watched Rebecca pale, her eyes widen. "With my brother," he said matter-of-factly.

Rebecca gave a slight gasp at the mention of James. She was unaware that anyone had noticed the kiss—it had happened so quickly after all. The afternoon sun suddenly felt scorching and Rebecca wiped at her brow. John smiled wickedly at her, but she was not about to give him the satisfaction of having surprised her. She cleared her throat and straightened her back, her face a mask as she locked eyes with John. "Yes, I kissed him goodbye on the cheek."

John resisted rolling his eyes. *She says it like it's normal,* he thought, *like it's something she's done a thousand times*. Suddenly a more frightening thought seized John—*what if she had done it a thousand times?* "Well, you've never done *that* before," he sputtered, hoping her reply would prove him correct.

"What of it?" she said cooly. "It was a simple kiss on the cheek. The very same kiss you give to your siblings, or your mother or father."

John was relieved at her response—he hated being left out, if James and Rebecca had shared kisses before, he expected to hear of it from both of them! Still, he didn't quite buy Rebecca's explanation. Sure, he had kissed his family members on the cheek before, but never a friend. Something told him this kiss meant something different, and he smiled wryly at Rebecca as he studied her.

As if John would understand, Rebecca thought. She crossed her arms and rolled her eyes at him. "You're making a big deal out of nothing," she huffed.

John remained silent and smiling, but he did not want to further upset his friend. He decided to change the subject. "You got an awful lot of compliments this morning at church," he hedged.

This was the wrong thing to say, the wrong subject to move to. Rebecca was annoyed. She felt like John was judging her for some wrong he felt she had done.

She shot up off the grass, hands in the air. "So, what of it!" Her arms were still crossed, her eyes narrowed into slits.

John stood and moved toward her, his voice low and apologetic. "I'm sorry, Becca. I didn't mean anything by it." He put a hand on her shoulder and felt her relax. "Honest. You deserve all the compliments. You really do."

"Thank you, John," she said. "That's kind of you to say." She walked back toward the brook, settling once more along its edge. John followed behind her. "Truthfully, the compliments make me uncomfortable."

John nodded. "They make me uncomfortable, too."

Rebecca's head snapped toward him, her eyebrows raised in confusion. John laughed. "Well, you're *our* friend, after all! Who do these boys think they are?"

Rebecca laughed, and John felt instantly better, his confidence returned. "And," he started, "it's just you've never kissed *me* on the cheek before."

Rebecca laughed even louder. "That's because your face is always dirty, John." Without hesitation, she scooped up a bit of mud from along the brook and smeared it on John's cheek. "See!"

They both had a good laugh and spent the rest of their time at the brook talking about the approaching Christmas season, which was still a few weeks away. And before it arrived, they, like James, had to return to their lessons.

The Southalls had hired a tutor—Mr. Philip Pender of Pennsylvania—to teach their older children at home, so John, and his younger sisters Frances and Elizabeth, along with his younger brother William, were taught a variety of subjects each day at the Raleigh. Rebecca's parents arranged for her to attend the lessons as well, so she and John spent time together nearly every day either at school, church, or sometimes at the brook, or on the porch of one of the taverns.

Although John never impressed Rebecca with his ability—or lack thereof—to learn dance steps, she *was* impressed with John's ability to understand Latin and Greek and his ferocious appetite to read books in those languages.

"Why don't you go to the college like James? You clearly have the ability." Rebecca said to John one day.

John was surprised by the question and replied with a shrug. "School has never interested me like it does James. I'd rather learn on my own. Too many silly rules over there."

Rebecca nodded in understanding. John was more of a free spirit than James. *He would certainly bristle at all the rules and probably get into endless trouble*, she thought. *Probably best that he didn't go to the college*.

James was away at school for his 15th birthday in early December, but he returned home a few days before Christmas and so the three friends were able to enjoy the Christmas season together. Nothing was said about the kiss—not because James had forgotten but rather, he was too shy to bring it up.

Neither the Southalls or the Andersons held a ball over Christmas, so there was no opportunity to dance, which disappointed Rebecca greatly. John also feigned disappointment that his 14th birthday at the end of December had not been marked by a ball at the Raleigh, which typically occurred every year after Christmas. Three years of war and the economic hardship caused by it had made it difficult for Mr. Southall to hold a Christmas ball in 1777.

Although the holiday season that year had been more subdued than usual, the three friends were able to enjoy their time together. Alas, when the new year started, the three friends separated once more as James had to return to school, and Rebecca enthusiastically, and John reluctantly, resumed their lessons with Mr. Pender at the Raleigh.

The Brook

18

The Raleigh Tavern

Chapter Two

No One Seems to Care Anymore

1778

The first two months of 1778 were rather uneventful in Williamsburg, but at the end of February, several Continental Army officers on furlough from Valley Forge visited the Raleigh Tavern. Eager for news, John lingered in the room that they dined in and listened as they discussed the challenges each faced to recruit new troops.

"It's impossible to find anyone to serve," complained a lieutenant.

"I'm ashamed of my countrymen," lamented another, several years older than the first but still in his twenties. "They seem not to care anymore about independence."

The complaints continued for another minute, riveting John's attention. He could not help but interject. "Perhaps," he said as he approached their table, "everyone thinks the war is already won because of Saratoga, and so they're no longer needed?"

The officers turned in their seats to face John, an awkward pause filling the air.

"Then they are sorely mistaken," barked the older lieutenant. "Our army at Valley Forge is a mere shadow of an army."

Feeling lucky that the officers had engaged with him, John seized upon the opportunity to continue the conversation, and perhaps learn more about life as a soldier. "Can you tell me more about the army, sir?"

The officers looked intently at John for a moment. "How old are you, lad?" asked the oldest looking one, a captain.

"Fourteen, sir."

They all frowned. Fourteen was too young to recruit.

"Well, lad," replied the captain, "the enlistments for many of our troops are about to expire, and I confess the past two years have been hard on them. Most are eager to return home, arguing it is time for others to step up and serve."

They are right about that, more should serve, John thought as he nodded in agreement.

"General Washington has offered furloughs to those who re-enlist," continued the officer, "so that they can go home for the winter. But to receive a furlough, they must re-enlist and return to the army in the spring to serve for three more years. Most are unwilling to do so."

"But do you really think the war will last three more years?" asked John, stunned at the thought.

"It won't last one more," the older lieutenant replied, "if we don't find new soldiers to recruit!"

"We'll find them," said the captain. "One way or another."

The previous year, Virginia's leaders had addressed the shortage of new recruits for the Continental Army by implementing a draft that would select men from each county militia. Each county was given a quota of men to send to Virginia's understrength regiments based on the county's size. In Williamsburg's case, the quota was just eight men.

The men selected had to be unmarried, older than eighteen, and have no children. If you were drafted, you would be expected to serve in the Continental Army for a year and would receive nearly $7 a month for pay (the equivalent of about $155 today), as well as a $15 ($335) bounty.

Unfortunately for General Washington and his Continental Army, Virginia's counties were slow to enact the draft, and so many of those drafted deserted before they reached Valley Forge. Therefore, Virginia's regiments remained extremely undermanned at Valley Forge.

John was troubled at the thought that his fellow Virginians were failing the army. He thought they should be the backbone of Washington's force.

"What's it like at Valley Forge?" he asked the officers.

"Well, son, the men are pretty well sheltered in huts," replied the captain, "and our defenses at Valley Forge are strong." He paused a moment, not sure whether it was wise to go any further, but John looked as if he was holding his breath with excitement, and the rum punch they were all drinking made the captain more talkative than he should have been. "I will tell you straight, lad," the captain sighed. "Our numbers are alarmingly low. The men sometimes go hungry for days. Many are dressed in rags, and many fall sick. It's not a pleasant situation, son."

John's stomach sank at the description. Just three months earlier he and the whole city had celebrated the news of Saratoga, and many had believed the end of the war was near. These officers, however, described a far different situation, and John wondered for the first time whether the patriots would even win the war.

It was then that the fourth officer at the table, who had been silent up to that point, spoke up. “Perhaps we can draw France into the war on our side. That would certainly shake things up, would it not?”

John smiled eagerly, grateful for the hope the comment provided. He looked expectantly at the captain, awaiting his reply.

“Indeed, it would,” said the captain, much to John’s relief. “And perhaps they *will* join us. But in the meantime, we must press on the best we can.” He fixed his attention back to John. “Be a good lad and fetch us more punch, will you?”

John nodded and went to refill their punch bowl.

Across the street at Mr. Anderson’s tavern, Rebecca overheard a similar discussion between two other American officers who had also been sent back to Virginia to recruit because there were so few Virginian troops at Valley Forge.

“I’ve had my fill of this war,” declared the younger of the two officers, both captains, over dinner.

“It seems the whole country has,” replied the other. “I’ll tell you truthfully though, I’m pleased to be back here rather than in camp.”

Anderson's Tavern

"Aye, me as well," replied the other officer. "And I suspect we may never return, for I doubt we will find enough men to command."

Rebecca did not engage the officers in conversation as John had. She merely listened to their discussion from the side of the room as she waited to assist them and the other guests in the dining room, silently gathering information to share with her friend.

"Things sound pretty bad for General Washington and his men," Rebecca told John when they met at the brook the next day. "It sounds like everyone is giving up on independence."

"I know," John sighed. "The officers I heard are discouraged about raising troops. I just can't understand why people would give up after we won at Saratoga just a few months ago."

"Everyone is tired, John. The war has gone on much longer than anyone expected."

As grim as the news from Valley Forge was, the American army managed to survive its winter encampment there. The situation slowly improved during the spring with the arrival of new recruits from several states, including Virginia, and the return of soldiers who had been furloughed over the winter.

When Virginia's General Assembly convened in Williamsburg in May, recruiting more troops for the Continental Army was a top priority. The legislators authorized the recruitment of two thousand new volunteers to serve with General Washington's army for just six months. To sweeten the deal, the volunteers were offered a bounty of $30 ($670)—double the bounty paid to those drafted from the militia. The volunteers were also promised a complete uniform and monthly pay. Few accepted the offer, however, and so Virginia remained well short of its Continental quota of recruits for 1778.

While Virginia's legislators met in the Capitol, exciting news arrived from Paris. Inspired by America's victory at Saratoga, France finally agreed to an alliance with America, pledging to assist the fledgling country in its struggle for independence from Great Britain. Most Virginians were relieved and excited by the news. Many hoped this new alliance would finally bring a successful conclusion to the war.

Rebecca was particularly relieved by the news. She had long worried that the war might eventually harm James and John—as well as her own father—as it had already harmed so many others over the last three years. She thus embraced the news of the alliance between America and France with great feelings of hope.

"Surely King George will realize the hopelessness of continuing the war now that France has joined our side," she declared to John as they talked about the alliance on the porch of the Raleigh.

"He ought to," agreed John. "We almost had them beat by ourselves. They can't possibly beat us now that France is with us."

I just hope it ends before more have to suffer and die, Rebecca thought to herself.

There was a lull in the conversation until John cleared his throat noisily. "So," he started awkwardly, "I noticed that Adam Craig has been visiting with you a lot lately,"

"How uncharacteristic of you," said Rebecca, "changing the subject *away* from the war."

John tilted his head sideways. "Uncharacteristic—"

"You need not worry about Mr. Craig," snapped Rebecca, careful to address him formally instead of by his given name. She did not want John to read into things and think she and Adam Craig were closer than they actually were.

But John simply smiled at her. "Oh, I'm not worried," he said. "Just making an observation."

Rebecca chose to ignore John's attempt to rile her and shifted the subject to James. "How is James doing at school?" she asked.

"I suppose he's doing fine." John shrugged. "Just one more month before he's home for the summer."

James returned home from school in mid-June and the three friends looked forward to another summer together. In July, exciting news of an important battle in New Jersey reached Williamsburg.

"We drove the British from Philadelphia and across New Jersey," John bragged to James and Rebecca after he'd heard the news in the tavern.

"General Washington does deserve credit," James replied, "but I think the British left Philadelphia more out of concern of the French than of General Washington."

John remained unfazed. "No matter," he said with a wave of his hand. "He still chased them across New Jersey and now they sit in New York like trapped rats."

The battle that the boys were talking about occurred near Monmouth Courthouse in New Jersey and was a significant clash. This day long battle—in which the American army attacked the rear of the British column leaving Philadelphia—ended in deadlock at nightfall with both armies still on the field. When the British withdrew during the evening, however, it signified to most Americans that they had won the battle.

Like the battles of Trenton and Princeton eighteen months earlier, and Saratoga just eight months ago, news of Washington's victory at Monmouth lifted American spirits.

"First Philadelphia, and next New York," predicted John. "We didn't even have any help from the French at Monmouth, just imagine what we can do when they actually join us."

James nodded in response but stayed quiet. Unlike his brother, James was not eager to go to war. Being just five months away from his 16th birthday, however, James knew that service in the militia was on the horizon. He wasn't worried about what might happen to him in the militia, but he was concerned about what he might be forced to *do* while serving. *I just don't know if I can kill another*, he thought to himself, embarrassed and ashamed of his doubt.

Chapter Three

Militia Service

1778-1779

The fourth summer of war passed rather uneventfully in Williamsburg after the exciting news of Monmouth. General Henry Clinton, the new British commander in North America, seemed content to remain inactive in New York, and General Washington could do little to threaten him without the aid of the French, which was slow to arrive.

In July, Mr. Pender—John and Rebecca's tutor—surprised everyone with his unexpected departure for Pennsylvania. The children wondered if the British evacuation of Philadelphia had something to do with his sudden decision, but he wouldn't say. "Private affairs at home require my immediate attention," was his only explanation.

"I miss his lessons," sighed Rebecca one hot August afternoon at the brook.

"Me too," John agreed, surprising his brother, who was cooling his feet in the water.

"You do?" asked James, unable to hide his astonishment.

"Certainly! I don't particularly miss the mathematics lessons, but I enjoyed Latin and Mr. Pender's stories of the ancient past. It was an interesting time back then."

"As it is for us now," replied James.

"I suppose it's harder to realize how important things are when you're in the middle of it all," speculated Rebecca. "I've heard many say we must continue to fight for posterity's sake."

John tilted his head. "Posterity?"

"Surely Mr. Pender taught you the meaning of the word posterity before he left," laughed James.

"One cannot be expected to remember every word uttered by his tutor," John countered.

Rebecca smiled at the two of them. "It means future generations, John. It is said that we must continue to fight so that those who come after us may have a brighter future."

John's eyes lit up. "Mr. Pender mentioned this a few times!" he said excitedly. "He said what we were doing by declaring our independence was something new and radical, not seen since the time of Greece and Rome, before the emperors."

"He probably meant the new governments we've created more than our break from Britain," said James. "There have been plenty of rebellions in the past. What makes this different is that we are now a republic, we have no King."

"Well aside from the fighting, life doesn't feel all that different from before," noted John. "We still have a governor, we still have an Assembly, and most of its members are the same men who were in the House of Burgesses. That doesn't sound very revolutionary."

"That may be true," replied James. "But some men are not the same and our governor is *elected* by the Assembly now—not appointed by the King. The people have more of a say in matters."

"And the King can't interfere with our laws like he used to," added Rebecca.

James walked a bit deeper into the brook, wanting to escape the summer heat. "I just hope the French King doesn't think his help entitles him to interfere with us in the future," James said. "The last thing we want is to trade one King for another—especially a *French* King."

All three laughed at the thought and James's attention shifted to Rebecca, to her smile, her bell-like laugh. He was so focused on her that he did not notice the rock beneath his feet and stumbled, sending water directly her way.

Rebecca gasped as the water soaked through her frock. The air stilled, everyone held their breath, James felt his heart stop and became increasingly worried that it would not restart.

When Rebecca saw the color of James's face—white as the ghosts rumored to be in her father's tavern—she knew what she had to do.

"It's just water, Becca, it won't hurt you," John said in an attempt to diffuse the tension.

But Rebecca was already acting on her plan and taking off her shoes and stockings as John spoke.

She flashed the brothers a mischievous grin. "Indeed, it is. So, you shouldn't mind this a bit." She sprung into the brook, splashing water in their direction.

John and James both let out a cry of protest and scrambled up the bank, laughing as they did. It was Rebecca who laughed the loudest and longest though.

Mr. Southall had hired another tutor for John's siblings in August, but John's formal lessons were over, as were Rebecca's. John did not mind the change, but Rebecca was disappointed. Her parents explained that the new tutor was not as qualified as Mr. Pender, so she had little to gain from his instruction. That may have been true, but a more likely reason was that the Andersons needed Rebecca to help look after and tutor her five-year old sister, Hope, as well as help with the operation of the tavern. She simply did not have time to study anymore—though her parents would never say so outright.

James returned to the college for his final year in September. Although he was three months shy of his 16th birthday, he joined the college's militia company. Formed in the summer of 1777, it amounted to about half the size of a typical militia company in Virginia with just over thirty members.

The new college president, Reverend James Madison, commanded the company. Governor Henry assigned him the rank of captain, but he was more of a figurehead than the company's actual commander. Reverend Madison's subordinate officers, two students at the college, Lieutenant William Nelson and 2nd Lieutenant Daniel

Fitzhugh, actually led the company. Despite a shortage of muskets that left more than half the company, including James, with only clubs to practice with, they met once a week behind the college to drill.

James marked his 16th birthday at the college and two weeks later returned home for Christmas break. The day after his return, a company of Williamsburg's militia mustered under the command of James's father for its monthly drill. James joined them with his father's permission.

John watched enviously from the sidelines and provided James with an assessment once the drill was over. "I thought you looked pretty good. Better than some but not quite as good as others."

"Thank you, brother. It felt strange to have a musket for once, even if the lock was broken."

"Father says most in the magazine are in poor shape, not of much use except to drill with."

James nodded. "I wish we had some of the damaged ones at school. I feel foolish carrying a big wooden club in the ranks."

"Do you march a lot when you drill at school?"

"Do we ever! A lot more than we did today. Our officers need as much practice giving commands as we do in executing them, and since its pretty useless to go through the manual of arms with clubs, we do a lot more marching and deploying."

"Father says that practicing the movements of a company is far more important than practicing the manual of arms. He says the movements are important in battle, while the manual of arms is more for show on the parade ground."

"He's right of course," said James. "I just suspect that many of his men prefer to limit the amount of marching they do at each muster."

John laughed and agreed. "Indeed, it takes quite an effort for some of them to march. Still," he paused, gazing longingly toward the empty drill field, "I envy them."

Later in the evening before the brothers turned in, James asked John how Rebecca was. He'd been home for several days but hadn't seen her yet.

John studied his brother, taking note of his reluctance to make eye contact, his determination to appear aloof, casual. John smiled to himself. "Oh, she's fine," he shrugged, trying to match James's nonchalant attitude.

"She doesn't have as many visitors as she used to. Or at least I haven't noticed them as much."

James did his best to hide his smile. "And she is well?"

"Oh sure, she is fine," said John, pausing before he added, "She's eager to see you again."

That statement set James's smile free. John grinned back at him, happy to see his older brother in such high spirits.

James had hoped to see Rebecca the next day, but his plans were disrupted when an alarm reached Williamsburg that a British fleet was off the coast.

"Here we go, lad," Captain Southall said to James as he passed him his coat. "We're forming at the magazine. John, you come too."

The boys grabbed their hats and followed their father toward the door, but stopped suddenly. Their mother stood in the doorway with a stern yet anxious look on her face.

"You boys listen to your father," she said before turning to John, her eyes sharp. "Especially you, John!"

John nodded solemnly. "Of course, Mother."

"And James," Mrs. Southall said turning to her husband, "you take care of yourself and my boys."

"I will, dear," replied Mr. Southall, kissing his wife on the cheek. "I'm sure this is nothing serious." He gave his wife's hand a squeeze and then dashed out the door.

"We'll be fine, Mother," whispered James in the doorway as he hugged her.

"You just do as your father says. And look after each other," she said as she hugged each of them.

The boys hurried to catch up to their father who had set a brisk pace up Duke of Gloucester Street. People were scurrying all about them, and the continuous clang of the church bell in the distance cast an ominous yet exciting mood.

When they reached the powder magazine, they found about half the company already there. Captain Southall worked his way through the assembled men and met with Colonel John Dixon, the printer and city alderman, who had overall command of both of Williamsburg's militia companies.

James and John stayed close by their father and overheard Colonel Dixon explain the cause of the alarm.

"We received a dispatch from Hampton this morning that a large British fleet was off the capes. They may be coming this way," said the colonel.

"Shall I form my company?" their father asked.

"Have Lieutenant Waller form yours and Lieutenant Russell form Captain Norton's; he should be here soon," said Colonel Dixon. "I need you to arm the men from the magazine. Eight rounds per man, captain."

"Yes, sir," their father replied, taking the magazine keys from the colonel. James and John followed their father into the magazine.

There were only thirty odd muskets stacked in a rack ready for use. Many others rested against the wall in disrepair. Some had broken springs on their locks and some had no locks at all. A handful of men arrived with their own weapons, but more than half of the men in Williamsburg's two militia companies—which numbered nearly a hundred men—would have to go unarmed because of all the damaged weapons.

"Fill each cartridge box with eight cartridges," their father said as he pointed to two small barrels full of musket cartridges. The leather cartridge boxes, which numbered over sixty, hung on pegs on the wall.

The boys grabbed a handful of boxes and brought them to a table next to the cartridges. A wooden block with twenty-four drilled holes was in each cartridge box. The wooden block and leather surrounding it were meant to protect the cartridges—filled with gunpowder and a lead musket ball—from damage, mostly from rain, but also from a wayward spark.

Eight rounds won't last very long, thought James as he and John hurriedly filled the boxes.

"Do you think you'll get a musket?" whispered John.

"I doubt it," James whispered back, "there are so few."

Their father led two men into the magazine and each took three muskets out of the room for distribution. Another man came in and took an arm load of cartridge boxes the boys had filled.

It only took a few minutes for the boys to fill all the cartridge boxes with eight rounds. And by then, all the working muskets in the magazine had been retrieved and distributed.

Their father looked over a list of those who received a musket, and a longer list of those who received a cartridge box. He signed both lists, then turned to the boys. "Come with me, lads."

John's heart leapt as it appeared he was about to join the militia a year earlier than the law called for. The boys followed their father, who had stopped before his company, about thirty-five men lined up in two lines. The front rank was largely armed but the rear rank had few weapons.

"James, take your position in the rear," his father said. "John, you stay close to me."

Lieutenant Waller approached Captain Southall and reported they were missing fifteen men, but most were expected soon.

Captain Southall nodded. "Very good, Lieutenant. Take your position now."

Captain Norton's company was still disorganized so Colonel Dixon focused his attention there. Captain Southall used the time to address his company. John stood back while his father spoke.

"Men," began Captain Southall, "we've been mustered because of a report that a British fleet is off our coast. We don't know if they intend to land here or elsewhere, but we need to be ready if Virginia is their destination."

James noticed that the mood among the men around him was far more serious than the previous day when they had mustered to drill. Many only half-heartedly drilled yesterday, and a few had even cracked jokes every chance they got. But now everyone listened intently to Captain Southall, and a sense of pride for his father welled up in James.

Colonel Dixon and Major Joseph Hornsby, his second in command, conversed with Captains Southall and Norton in front of the two companies. John remained near the troops, as did James, who stood in the rear rank, unarmed.

After a few minutes, the captains returned to their companies and took their places on the right end of their front ranks. Colonel Dixon faced both companies with his sword drawn and yelled, "Battalion! Attention!" Both companies fell silent and snapped to attention.

"You all likely know by now why we are mustered here, and I thank you all for your diligence in reporting for duty," started Colonel Dixon. "A strong enemy fleet has been sighted near the capes and there is concern that Virginia is its destination. Militia are turning out all along the Tidewater, and if the enemy is foolish enough to approach, I am confident we will give them a warm reception."

James and John shared the same thought: *How warm could the reception be when more than half of the militia is unarmed and those with muskets only have eight shots*?

The Powder Magazine

"Until we know more about the enemy's intentions," continued Colonel Dixon, "we will post ourselves inside the courthouse to get warm. Captains, take charge of your men!"

Both captains ordered their men to break ranks and reform inside the courthouse, which the men happily complied with. Most leaned against the walls and some sat on the floor, but all were grateful to be out of the cold and wind as the day slowly passed with no further word.

Around sunset, it was decided to send the troops home with the understanding that they were to assemble at the courthouse as quickly as possible upon the ringing of the church bell.

The night passed peacefully, and then the next day, still with no further word on the British fleet. Unbeknownst to the inhabitants of Williamsburg, it had sailed past Virginia on its way to Georgia, where three thousand British troops would soon land and seize Savannah before the year ended.

Although the Virginians were relieved to be spared from direct conflict, the presence of a powerful British fleet in the south in 1778 marked a new strategy for the British—one that brought the enemy closer to Virginia.

This realization created a somber mood in Williamsburg during the Christmas season. The war had long been a distant affair to most Virginians, a bloody conflict hundreds of miles away. But now it seemed it could arrive in Virginia at any moment.

"We're not ready!" lamented John, when he, James, and Rebecca gathered upon the Raleigh Tavern's porch on New Year's Day. "How can we possibly fight them with so few weapons and powder?"

"Father says General Washington needs to send the Virginian troops home to protect us," said Rebecca.

"I'm not sure he can afford to do that," replied James. "I hear his army is pretty small again."

John sighed, his head in his hands. "Well, the French have certainly been no help."

"Maybe they've done things behind the scenes," said James.

John rolled his eyes. "Perhaps. But rather than wait for them to do more, we need to prepare to defend ourselves."

Rebecca sat quietly as the boys discussed what needed to be done. Her father had said similar things at dinner the previous day, and it saddened her to think that all those she loved were closer to war than ever before.

James's voice brought her out of her thoughts. "You've been very quiet, Becca. Is anything the matter?"

She gave him a sheepish smile and shook her head. "Just concerned about what might happen next."

"I wouldn't worry," declared John. "I don't think the British have enough men to bother us *and* keep New York. If any arrive here, I expect it will be just a raid."

"Raids could still do a lot of damage," chided James. "And you saw last week how ill prepared we are to fight."

John folded his arms defensively. "Well, I just don't think the British are strong enough to attack us here and still keep New York is all I'm saying,"

James grinned at his brother, admiring his optimism. "Let's hope you're right."

Rebecca cleared her throat, ready for a change of subject. "Are you ready for your last term, James?"

"I am indeed," he replied. "Just one more term, then my examinations and I shall be a graduate of the college."

"That's quite impressive," Rebecca smiled. "I'm proud of you."

"Thank you, Becca. That means a great deal to me." Each blushed and looked down at their feet.

As much as John cared for his brother and Rebecca, and was aware something was different between them, conceding that Rebecca was smitten with James was difficult. He stood between them, commanding both their gazes as he shook his hands in the air. "Yes, yes, we're all proud of you James. But have you two forgotten that next week is my 15th birthday? This will be the *second* year that we don't celebrate it with a ball!" he cried.

James and Rebecca smiled at each other and then at John, all three aware that the annual Christmas balls had nothing to do with John's birthday

"Well, I guess Father figures fifteen isn't really that important of a birthday for a ball," joked James.

"Besides," added Rebecca, "it's not like you ever enjoyed dancing."

"That's not true!" John protested. "I enjoyed dancing with you at last year's ball."

"For two dances," countered James.

Rebecca patted John's arm, coming to his defense. "And you danced wonderfully."

John shook her hand off. "I couldn't help it that you were in such demand, Becca. It was nearly impossible to get your attention, much less steal you away for another dance."

James smiled to himself as he thought back to the ball. He had managed to dance with Rebecca more than anyone there, and he knew that it was by *her* choice that he managed to do so. James had always felt close to Rebecca—she was his best friend—but their first ball together had changed things between them.

She was more than just a friend after the ball; she was on his mind all the time at school, and he was eager to finish his studies so that he could spend more time with her. The reports from John of a parade of boys visiting Rebecca over the past year concerned James, and despite that sudden kiss on the cheek she had bestowed on him, he wasn't sure that she was as fond of him as he was for her—but he hoped so.

John already knew the answer. He suspected it the moment the kiss happened, but felt the truth of it when Rebecca had thrown herself into the brook to save James from embarrassment. He knew, just as Rebecca knew, that when she arrived home that day, she would be scolded for ruining her frock. But she had leapt into the water anyway.

Rebecca was always polite to the other boys who visited her, but John could tell they bored her. They were simply charming distractions, placeholders until James returned from school. John knew Rebecca's heart had settled on James.

At first this realization had saddened John. He worried that he was going to lose both his brother and Rebecca, that they would no longer want him around and he would be left alone. But he had fought hard to silence those thoughts, for nothing in their manner hinted that that was a possibility. The three friends were as close as ever.

But then he had also, strangely, felt a surge of anger, with a deep undercurrent of shame, like he had somehow lost a contest to his brother. He dismissed that feeling quickly. He knew deep down that James was far better suited for Rebecca than he was. *He's always been a much better dancer than I,* he thought with a chuckle. And while Rebecca was beautiful and kind, John had only ever seen her as a friend.

He had no time for love anyway. War had come to the South and he was just a year away from militia service. For John, there were much bigger issues to focus on than love.

Chapter Four

The College Company Marches
1779

Despite the disturbing news of the fall of Savannah to the British at the end of 1778, hope for a patriot victory started to grow in early 1779 with reports that Holland and Spain were soon to declare war against Britain.

John and Rebecca discussed the exciting news one warm spring day at the brook.

"If the news is true, I can't see how Britain continues to fight much longer," said Rebecca.

"They won't!" John insisted. "They couldn't beat us when we were alone, so they surely haven't a chance when France, Spain, and Holland are on our side."

"Well, I don't see how France has helped us very much," Rebecca muttered.

John nodded. "It's been disappointing, I admit, but the redcoats *did* abandon Philadelphia when they learned of the alliance. And except for going to Savannah, they've been pretty quiet in New York. Maybe James was right, maybe the French have helped us more than we know."

Rebecca considered this. “Yes, I suppose they have. So, if France has made Britain less aggressive, maybe Spain and Holland joining us might convince them to let us go?”

“Let’s hope so,” said John, surprising Rebecca with his agreement. “I’m ready to see this war end. Four years is long enough.”

Rebecca grinned, happy that John finally seemed to understand the seriousness of war. “Four years is certainly long enough.”

It was likely the monthly musters with his father’s militia company—and their lack of arms and equipment—that had swayed John’s opinion about war. Although he was still nearly a year away from sixteen, his father, Captain Southall, had allowed John to participate in the militia drills held at the magazine. He had been issued one of the broken muskets for practice, which disappointed him, but he did enjoy being in the ranks under his father’s command. And ever since the alarm in December and news of the fall of Savannah, there was a higher level of seriousness among all the participants at drill that made John realize that this was not a game.

John and Rebecca's hope that Britain might soon accept American independence and end the war was dashed in May, however, when General Henry Clinton, the British commander in New York, sent an expeditionary force of one thousand eight hundred troops to raid Virginia. The troops arrived on May 8th, aboard twenty-two transport ships. Six powerful warships escorted the transports. The largest, the H.M.S. *Raisonable* with sixty-four cannons, anchored off Hampton while the bulk of the expedition sailed up the Elizabeth River and landed troops at Portsmouth.

The General Assembly had been in session and Williamsburg was crowded with legislators and visitors when news of the British expedition arrived. Governor Henry, nearing the end of his third and final term as governor, immediately called out the militia and within days hundreds of troops from nearby counties had arrived in the city.

It was decided that some troops would be sent to Hampton, and Williamsburg's two militia companies were selected to go. Captain Southall shared the news with his family, then pulled John aside.

"John," he said sternly, "I can't have you come with us, it would serve no purpose, we haven't enough weapons."

John was devastated, and a sense of shame swept over him. He opened his mouth to protest but his father cut him off, his hand heavy on John's shoulder. "Son, I know you are ready and eager to go—"

"I am, Father, I—" John started as he reached up and grabbed his father's wrist.

Mr. Southall steadied his son with a level gaze. "But I need you here with your mother," he said firmly. "In case the enemy appears while we are gone. Your mother will need your help with your brothers and sisters if that happens, and it very well could. I'm counting on you, John."

Disappointment still lingered, but his father's confidence in him boosted John's spirits a bit. He gave his father a curt nod. "I understand, Father. You can count on me."

The Williamsburg militia marched to Hampton the following day. The college company—some twenty-five student-soldiers including James—also took the field. Their destination was not Hampton, however, but

Smithfield, a town across the James River in Isle of Wight County.

After the British landed in Portsmouth, a portion of their force marched to Suffolk, twenty miles away, and burned the town. Militia were gathering in Smithfield, about twenty miles north of Suffolk, to oppose the British if they continued northward. The college company, led by Lieutenant William Nelson, was attached to the Charles City County militia and joined other companies in a march to Smithfield.

As they were ferried across the river at Jamestown, James and his comrades stared intently down river, anxious about the possible appearance of enemy warships. Four years of war had created a severe shortage of clothing in Virginia, so the college company, like the other militia companies with them, were not uniformly dressed. Most wore light linen coats and breeches of different colors with an assortment of tricorn and round hats. All of the college company carried muskets and cartridge boxes, but they had just one flint each and no cartridges for their boxes. The hope was that they would find a supply of cartridges when they reached Smithfield. Furthermore, fifteen of the youngest members of the company were left behind at the college because there were not enough muskets for them.

James was one of the leaders in the company, not by rank, but by reputation. His height placed him in the rear rank of the company, but his serious yet patient demeanor and willingness to help others with the drill, won him the respect of all.

"Are you ready for this, James?" asked Isaac Hite, a second-year student in the college from Frederick County in the Shenandoah Valley. "Do you think we're really going to fight the redcoats?"

"I don't know, Isaac," James said as he looked warily down river. "But I think we're ready if we have to. Just remember the drill and listen to the officers."

They landed at Cobham late in the day and camped along the shore. Gathered around small fires to cook the cornmeal they brought with them, the young soldiers gobbled down hoecakes and speculated on what lie ahead.

"I only see about two hundred men with us," said Isaac. "Do you think that is enough to stop the British?"

"There will be others at Smithfield when we arrive," James assured him. "And we'll find some cartridges too. Don't worry."

“This hasn’t been bad so far,” said Mordecai Cooke, a second-year student from Yorktown. “The stories one hears from those up north with General Washington make war seem pretty bad, but this hasn’t been like that at all.”

“Speak for yourself,” grumbled Phillip Ramsey, a first-year student from Norfolk County. “My feet are killing me.”

“We only marched seven miles today,” said Thomas Hall, another second-year student from Louisa County.

“Well, that’s six miles more than I’m used to,” griped Phillip.

“You better brace yourself for tomorrow then because we’ve got a lot further to go,” James warned.

“Has anyone ever been to Smithfield?” asked Johnson Tabb, a third-year student from Elizabeth City County.

“I’ve never been across the river,” replied James, to the laughter of the group.

The talk continued until dark when the tired student-soldiers finally succumbed to sleep, wrapped in their blankets under the stars.

They awoke abruptly to yelling. “Get up boys! Get up and prepare to march,” shouted a sergeant from Charles City County.

"But what about breakfast?" protested Phillip.

"You should have cooked that last night," snarled the sergeant, who was a veteran of the Continental Army during the first years of the war. "There's no time now! Let's go!"

The boys reluctantly rose and prepared for the march. The sun had just risen and the morning was cool and fresh.

This won't be so bad, thought James as he rolled up his wool blanket and crammed it in his pack. He reached for his musket and noticed a bright film of orange rust on the barrel and edges of his lock. He and the others had left their muskets uncovered, and all now had an orange film of rust on them, courtesy of the morning dew.

The gruff sergeant who had awakened them re-appeared and glared disapprovingly at the muskets.

"This won't do, lads! You need to care for your muskets and cover them at night." He turned from them and shouted, "Corporal Evans, bring the bottle of sweet oil and some patches. These boys have work to do." He turned back to the boys, his eyes still narrowed, his tongue sharp. "Ten minutes, you have ten minutes to clean your muskets and prepare to march!"

Lieutenant Nelson had joined the gaggle at that point and looked annoyed. *Who is this usurper giving orders to my troops?* he thought. He said nothing though because the sergeant was right.

James and his comrades scrambled to clean their muskets. The rust came off with the application of a few drops of sweet oil upon a cloth patch and a lot of rubbing.

College Company

"When we get to Smithfield you can clean them better with brick dust and make them shine," said the sergeant, "but this will do for now."

Most had finished with their muskets before the lone drummer in the detachment beat assembly and the men formed their companies.

Captain John Carter commanded the Charles City County Company and he placed the college company as a separate platoon on the left of his line.

The entire detachment was under the command of Major Alexander Harrison, who ordered the companies to right face. Everyone turned a quarter turn to the right and waited for the next command. "Forward march," shouted Major Harrison, prompting the column of soldiers to begin their long march to Smithfield.

The sun had already risen above the trees when they began, and as they marched, James noticed cleared fields on both sides of the sandy road with hundreds of small tobacco and corn hills scattered among scores of tree stumps and dead trees. Off in the distance, enslaved men and women worked with hoes to break and hill new ground. They took no notice of the column of troops marching south to Smithfield.

At first there was a lot of chatter in the ranks, but that died down before they could complete the first mile. The column halted to rest after an hour of marching, but were soon at it again.

By early afternoon they had marched twelve miles and some of the boys protested that they could go no further—their feet ached and were swollen with blisters. But just as they were about to fall out, the column halted and the officers gathered. It was decided to rest for a couple of hours and complete the march in the late afternoon.

Lieutenant Nelson informed his troops. "Take your shoes off and treat those blisters as best you can. We still have eight miles to go, but we're going to stay here for a few hours." The lieutenant turned to James. "Mr. Southall," he said, "form a detail to gather wood for cooking fires."

James was surprised at his assignment, but jumped to action quickly with a "yes, sir!" James turned to the weary company. All were sitting, and all refused to meet his gaze.

James sighed. He knew they were tired—so was he—but an order was an order. "I think three volunteers should do it," he said to the trees, as if he were talking only to himself and not the exhausted boys. There was an awkward pause before three lads finally hoisted themselves up and volunteered.

"We don't need much wood for cooking fires, let's just gather the deadfall lying about," James instructed. Each gathered an armful and returned to find their comrades all massaging their feet and tending to their blisters.

James's own blisters throbbed, but he did his best to ignore them. "Let's get the fires started for them," he said, "they'll return the favor in due course."

It was another pleasant May afternoon in Virginia and the boys thoroughly appreciated their chance to rest and eat.

Realizing that they were still several hours away from Smithfield and that by the time they arrived it might be difficult to cook a meal, James suggested that they cook enough hoecakes and salt pork for their dinner—which they ate while they rested—as well as for supper and breakfast tomorrow.

Tired as they were, everyone agreed it was a good idea, even though the hoecakes would likely turn to crumbs in their pockets while they marched.

Better crumbs than nothing, thought James.

At four o' clock the sergeant was at it again, yelling for everyone to put out the fires and prepare to march. They were on the road within fifteen minutes, but several of the company could not march any further and soon fell out. They were joined by a number of men from other companies who also had trouble with their feet.

The column halted and the officers gathered to decide what to do. After much discussion, they decided to allow the men who could march no further to halt for the rest of the day and continue to Smithfield tomorrow morning.

James was not privy to the officers' discussion. While he waited for their decision, he took in the natural beauty of a spring afternoon in the Virginia countryside, trying to place the species of a bird he'd spotted in a nearby tree—a sparrow perhaps, or maybe a warbler. *Mr. Wythe would certainly know*, thought James. Before he had settled the question, Lieutenant Nelson approached him.

"Mr. Southall," he said, clapping James on the back and drawing him close, his voice low. "I need you to stay behind and look after those who can no longer march."

Once again, James was surprised by the attention, but he nodded swiftly. "Certainly, sir."

"I expect you'll join us in Smithfield by noon," added Lieutenant Nelson.

"Of course, sir," replied James.

Two of the volunteers who had gathered wood during the long break in the afternoon also stayed behind to assist the dozen members of the college company who could march no more.

"Mr. Southall will look after you men, listen to him," announced Lieutenant Nelson before he rejoined the remnants of the company still able to march. "We'll see you tomorrow."

Although James did not hold a formal rank within the company, those left behind accepted his authority out of respect for him. There was no one in the college company, save the officers, who served with more seriousness or dedication, and the tired soldiers appreciated this now that they were actually in the field.

Captain Martin Price of New Kent County stayed behind to command everyone who remained.

"This is a fine spot to stay until morning," he said to James and the several officers and sergeants who had gathered around him to receive instructions. "If it rains we can use the woods right there," he pointed south of the road, "as shelter. Send a man into the wood line to see if there is a brook back there for the men to soak their feet. How are you all set for food?"

Several replied that they had enough food for another day, but others said their men needed to cook. James smiled, glad that he had convinced his comrades to cook extra food during the long halt.

"Mr. Southall," Captain Price called suddenly, "how fares your father?"

"He and my mother and siblings are all fine, sir."

A small smile broke across the captain's face. "I see you do not recognize me, son," he continued. "It *has* been some time since I've seen you at the Raleigh."

James stared more intently at Captain Price but could not place him. So many men frequented the tavern, after all. "I've been at the college for some time, sir," replied James, as way of apology. "I complete my studies this term."

Captain Price nodded his approval. "Very good, well done."

Just then a sergeant came up and asked where he should have the sinks dug for the men to relieve themselves. Captain Price bowed to James, then led the sergeant to the desired spot.

James returned to his comrades, who were all sitting with their shoes and stockings off, many gingerly examining their blisters.

"Should I pop it or leave it be?" asked John Morrison. "This one is so squishy."

James wasn't usually squeamish around such things, but the sight of John's blister made his stomach turn. "I think maybe it's best to leave it alone," he said. "If it's meant to pop it will pop."

"Hey!" A voice shouted out from the trees. "There's a brook just inside the woods!" The boys all looked at each other, unsure whether they should, or even *could,* make their way to the brook on their sore feet.

James glanced up at the boys, noting the concern in their eyes. They knew that pain awaited them as soon as they tried to stand and limp to the brook. "Ah, let's let the others soak their feet first. They won't be long," he said. The boys sighed with relief and agreed.

The footsore student-soldiers eventually did find the resolve to make the walk to the brook and James accompanied them, eager to soak his own sore feet for a bit. The water was cold and their blisters stung at first, but eventually their feet became numb, which was what everyone desired.

James helped John Morrison and his squishy blisters back to the camp, which had been placed on the edge of the woods by Captain Price. James suggested that everyone who could still walk gather deadfall for a campfire. After, the boys laid out their blankets with their feet toward the fire and feasted on the hoecakes they had cooked up hours earlier.

Sleep came fast for James and his comrades, but after midnight the temperature dropped and it began to rain lightly. James and the others, rolled up in their wool blankets with their muskets, but with no tents for shelter, tried to ignore the cold and rain, but their blankets grew damp and they spent the pre-dawn hours shivering restlessly in the darkness.

The rain continued into the morning, postponing their march and maintaining their misery. It finally ended around noon and Captain Price announced that it was time to march.

There was no effort to keep formation on the march, and the column was soon strung out for a quarter of a mile.

They stopped every mile or so to rest and allow stragglers to catch up, and ended up reaching Smithfield with only an hour of daylight remaining.

Lieutenant Nelson greeted James and the rest of the college company when they arrived. “Welcome back, boys. We missed you.” He strode toward James and patted him on the shoulder. “Well done, James. You kept everyone together.”

“They heard there was a good meal waiting for them here,” James said with a smile.

Lieutenant Nelson laughed and patted James on the shoulder once more. “If it were only so. Our accommodations,” he said as he pointed to a large barn nearby, “for the time being.”

James grinned at the sight of the barn, relieved for the shelter from future rain.

The college company remained in Smithfield for over a week. The townsfolk were grateful for the presence of all the troops and supplied them with fresh corn bread and meat daily.

“See, I told you army life wasn’t so bad,” joked Mordecai.

The other boys laughed in agreement. The hospitality of the townsfolk certainly helped fade the memories of painful blisters and dreary rain.

On their eighth day in town, Colonel Robert Lawson formed the troops—now over a thousand strong—and announced that the British had re-boarded their ships and had sailed from Portsmouth. Concerned that they might sail up the river to surprise them at Smithfield, he doubled the nightly picket guards. All the troops remained on high alert in Smithfield overnight.

The following afternoon, however, Colonel Lawson assembled the men again and announced that the British had sailed out to sea. The troops erupted in cheers.

After the last of three huzzas were shouted, Colonel Lawson ordered the troops to draw the rations they needed to return to their homes and cook them that afternoon. James and his comrades drew three days rations of cornmeal and salt pork. But by the time they finished cooking it all, it was too late to begin their march, so they waited until the next morning, heading toward the ferry at Cobham.

The pace of the return march was not as grueling as the march to Smithfield, and they halted frequently to rest, so it took two full days to reach Cobham. But the troops were better off for the slower pace.

It was too dark to safely cross the river that evening, so they camped on the shore and crossed early the next morning. A few more miles of marching from Jamestown put them back at the college in time for dinner.

It was a tired company of soldiers who returned to the college in late May. Reverend Madison briefly addressed the company on their return, announced that classes would resume in two days, then dismissed them so that they could eat and rest.

Everyone slept soundly for the first time in over a week, and James did not rise until mid-morning the next day—the day of Rebecca's 15th birthday.

The Southalls had planned to go and visit James at school that day and Rebecca, desperate to see James again, had asked if she could join. Of course, they emphatically agreed.

"Hail, Caesar!" John cried when he saw his brother. "Home from his first victorious campaign." John playfully bowed low before James—who looked at him disapprovingly—before he straightened and embraced

James with a hug. “Welcome back brother, we were worried about you.”

Everyone gathered around James and peppered him with questions. He assured them that everything went well.

“It was mostly a lot of marching and waiting. They never even issued us rounds.”

“That’s because they expected you to use the bayonet!” John declared, pretending to thrust an invisible bayonet toward James.

“Well, they would have been disappointed,” James chuckled. “For there’s not a bayonet to be found in the entire company.”

Everyone laughed and his mother made her way forward to hug James.

Rebecca stood off to the side, smiling.

James caught sight of her and stepped toward her. “Well, hello birthday girl. Happy 15th year.”

Rebecca was surprised that James remembered. He had been through quite an ordeal. She couldn’t imagine how tired he must be, and yet he still managed to remember her birthday.

“I’m sorry I do not have a present for you,” James said sheepishly.

But Rebecca launched herself forward into his arms. "Oh, James, *this* is the best present I could ever imagine."

College of William and Mary

Chapter Five

Graduation
1779

Just two weeks after Rebecca's 15th birthday, the Southalls and Rebecca gathered again at the college to celebrate James's graduation. Reverend Madison was highly complementary of James, but the comments James most appreciated were from his friend, fellow graduate, and commander in the college company—seventeen-year-old Lieutenant William Nelson.

"You're getting a fine soldier, sir," William said to Mr. Southall after the ceremony. "The entire company will miss him."

James waved the praise away. "You're the one they're going to miss, Will. You've led them for two years now."

"Couldn't have done it without you, James," countered William. "You were always steady as a rock. Someone I could truly rely on. Don't know why we never made you an ensign or sergeant."

"Because rank doesn't matter to him," John chimed in. "No one is humbler than James."

"Well, no question the company was better with him a part of it, and they will surely miss him."

The two young graduates bowed to each other and then William departed.

John leaned close to his brother. "And to think people like William used to bully you," he whispered. "Well done, brother."

Mr. Southall held a small entertainment in honor of all the graduates that evening in the Apollo Room of the Raleigh. Rebecca and her family attended, as did most of the graduates and their families, and most of the college faculty as well. It was a grand evening of music and dancing, but in the adjoining Daphne Room, a serious topic was under discussion.

The state legislature had just voted to move the capital from Williamsburg to somewhere further in the interior of the state—a decision prompted by the recent British raid on Virginia and the election of Thomas Jefferson as governor.

Although the measure had passed the General Assembly and Governor Jefferson supported it, most people in Williamsburg disbelieved that the move would actually occur.

"How can they afford to make such a move?" Mr. Anderson asked to a small gathering huddled around a card table. "There's no place in the interior that is suitable for a capital, and moving it to Fredericksburg or Alexandria would not appease the western counties who want it moved closer to them. I just can't see them actually going through with it," he insisted.

"I hope you're right, Robert," Mr. Southall replied. "Because if the government leaves, business will surely suffer."

Mrs. Southall arrived to break up the gathering. "Gentlemen," she said, her voice stern, "now is not the time to discuss politics. Now is the time to celebrate our new class of graduates. Come, Mr. Southall," she reached for her husband's arm, "let us return to them."

The gentlemen paused for a moment, then dutifully rose from the table to follow Mrs. Southall back to the Apollo room to enjoy the music and dancing.

Meanwhile, James chatted in the doorway with the parents of one of his fellow graduates. He was doing his best to divide his attention between the conversation and the dance, sneaking glances upon the dance floor in search of Rebecca. As he did so, General Thomas Nelson suddenly appeared before him, accompanied by his nephew, William. James smiled, happy to see his friend again.

"Mr. Southall," General Nelson said, "William says you were indispensable on the march to Smithfield. My compliments, sir."

"Thank you, sir," James replied with a formal bow, "but it was Lieutenant Nelson who has been indispensable to the company for the last two years."

General Nelson laughed, patted James on the shoulder, and turned to his nephew. "I see what you mean William, humble to a fault. "Well," the general continued, turning back to James, "it appears you've inherited your father's leadership skills." General Nelson nodded toward Mr. Southall, who stood next to his son, beaming with pride. "I congratulate you on a fine son, scholar, and soldier, sir."

As much as James appreciated the praise and attention lavished on him by General Nelson and others, he longed to be away from them and on the dance floor with Rebecca. As one of the guests of honor, however, he felt obligated to mingle with his well-wishers.

John tried his best to fill James's shoes and dance with Rebecca, but he had plenty of competition. Rebecca continued to be exceedingly popular among the boys.

She danced with several young men once or twice over the course of the evening, unable to decline their requests for fear of appearing rude. John danced with her four times, and James managed to escape onto the floor with her on three occasions—including the last dance. She had to ignore two suitors and interrupt James in the middle of a conversation to secure him for the last dance though. *Manners be damned*, she thought.

Rebecca could tell James was only half-listening to the conversation he was engaged in anyway—his eyes had glazed over and his smile was unnaturally tight. He noticeably relaxed when Rebecca approached him for the dance. "Thank you for saving me, Becca," he said as they took their places on the dance floor.

"Anything for our scholar and war hero," joked Rebecca with a smile.

At the end of the dance, Mr. Southall stepped into the center of the room and thanked everyone for attending, inviting them to stay as long as they wished.

Some continued to chat and play games, but most—including Mr. and Mrs. Anderson—thanked Mr. Southall for a lovely evening and said goodnight.

Rebecca, however, was not ready to leave and asked if she could stay a bit longer.

"I'll walk her home," James offered.

Mr. Anderson regarded his daughter and James. The pair seemed to be lit from within, their proximity to one another washing them both in happiness. He nodded to James. "Very good. But do not stay out too late, Rebecca."

Rebecca curtsied gratefully. "I won't, Father."

James and Rebecca mingled with the few guests who lingered behind, including John, who was listening intently to two gentlemen argue about the value of France's help in the war.

When things had quieted down, James asked if Rebecca would like to get some air. "Shall we take a stroll?" he suggested.

Rebecca took him by the arm. "Certainly," she replied. They walked out the front door and turned left, away from her house, which was just across the street.

James was happy to have Rebecca all to himself, but he was also enormously nervous. He racked his brain for conversation topics, before finally settling on one. "What was it like here while we were gone?"

"Pretty hectic actually," replied Rebecca. "The Assembly was still in session, and hundreds of soldiers arrived and milled about town for days. John seemed very pleased by their presence and talked quite a bit with them. I spent a lot of time tending to the officers who stayed with us."

James nodded. "Sounds like you were very busy."

Rebecca smiled at him. "Yes, I was. But not too busy to think of you."

James flushed a deep red and was grateful for the darkness. "R-really?" he sputtered.

"Really. I prayed for you every night and worried about you each day. But from what I overheard tonight," she continued, "it sounds like you were an excellent soldier. I'm not at all surprised."

"I am. I thought John was the soldier in the family. Well, he and my father. I guess I did all right. Though it wasn't what I thought it would be."

"In what way?"

James paused, considering this. He had thought there would be more action, that things would move at an alarmingly fast pace, that there would be no time to sit and ponder much of anything. The entire experience had been much slower than he anticipated.

"We didn't do any fighting. Heck, we didn't even draw any ammunition. We were unloaded the entire time we were in the field. We mostly marched and waited in camp for orders. It was exciting at first, but once we got to Smithfield it grew," he paused to lower his voice, "dull. I was very pleased when we finally started back for home."

Rebecca gave a small laugh. "If you have to take the field again, I hope you have the same experience. I want it to be the most uneventful time of your life."

James smiled and took her hand, squeezing it gently to acknowledge that he understood her and was thankful for her kindness. If they were merely friends, Rebecca would remove her hand from his at this point, but she tightened her grip.

They followed the Capitol circle around in silence until they were on Rebecca's side of the street. The silence continued until they reached the front of her father's tavern.

Rebecca finally removed her hand from James's to give him a playful curtsy. "Thank you for walking me home, kind sir."

James returned the gesture with an exaggerated bow. "It was a pleasure, my lady."

They stood staring at each other for a moment and then, as if possessed, James stepped forward and embraced Rebecca, kissing her on the lips. He tore himself away quickly, shocked at his own actions.

Rebecca stood silent, which only heightened James's alarm. "Forgive me if I was too forward. I…I…"

As James continued to sputter, Rebecca leaned forward and returned the kiss, standing on her toes and wrapping her arms around his neck. All panic gone, James embraced her and held her close. Rebecca snuggled her face into his shoulder, not wanting the moment to end.

When it did, she smiled at James and said, "Welcome home, graduate," before quickly scampering up the steps, turning back to him as she reached the door. "Good night, James." She opened the door and disappeared inside.

James stood at the bottom of the stairs elated at what had just occurred. *So, this is what love feels like*, he thought as he turned to head home. *I like this feeling. I like it a lot.*

James's graduation was old news by morning, replaced by the arrival of a notorious war criminal, Governor Henry "Hair Buyer" Hamilton. He had been captured months earlier far out west by Colonel George Rogers Clark and brought back to Williamsburg in chains. Accused of paying the natives who lived west of the Ohio River for the scalps of white settlers, Governor Hamilton was one of the most hated men in Virginia. He was brought to the jail and held in chains for months—a treatment not normally afforded a gentleman of his rank and stature. All of Williamsburg was excited by his arrival, and John wanted to go to the jail to see him. Rebecca and James, however, weren't interested.

"It's not like they'll have him out on display," James said to his brother. "Let the vile creature alone. He'll receive his just punishment."

About a week after James's graduation, a letter arrived at the tavern for him. It was his first letter, delivered by his friend William Nelson on behalf of his uncle, General Nelson. James shot his friend a puzzled look, but William merely shrugged, smiling. James opened the letter.

June 18, 1779

Dear Sir,

My wife and I congratulate you once again on the completion of your studies at the college and wish to inquire of your services. We shall be in need of a tutor in September for several of our children, and my nephew William assures us that you are more than suitable for the position. If you are interested, I should like to discuss the matter with you on my next visit to the city.

I Remain,

Your Most Obedient Servant,

T. Nelson

James stared back at William, mouth agape.

"Well, are you interested?" William laughed.

"What exactly does it entail?" James asked, his brow creased. "Your uncle has a number of children."

"I don't know the specifics, but I believe he wants you to tutor Philip, Francis, Hugh and Elizabeth. Philip is thirteen, Elizabeth nine, and the others fall in between."

James tried to imagine himself as a tutor. *Surely it could be no worse than tutoring John*, he thought. Tutoring John had been a challenging endeavor—so much so that

James had given up relatively quickly. *Still,* he thought, *that was because of John, not me.*

William waved a hand in front of James. “So,” he said, “are you interested?”

James found himself nodding. “Yes, yes I am. But I shall have to discuss it with my father.”

“Of course,” said William. “You have plenty of time. Uncle Thomas won’t be in town until next week, and the current tutor is staying on into September.”

“Fine, fine,” James replied distractedly. “That’s more than enough time to consider.”

At first, James told only his father about the offer. Mr. Southall heartily approved of any arrangement that placed his eldest son in the company of General Nelson.

“This is a fine thing, James, a very fine thing,” said Mr. Southall. “Surely you will accept it.”

“I think so father, but…but… There are things to consider.”

“What things?” asked his father incredulously. “How can you decline such an offer? General Nelson is the most important man in the county, and certainly one of the most important men in the state. How can you justify disappointing him?”

“Well…” stalled James, “Yorktown is quite far, a full day’s walk away, so I would be away from the city for quite some time.”

Mr. Southall gawked at his son. “And that is a problem because?”

“With all that is happening here, and the possible move of the government, and, and…”

“And what?” snapped his father, impatient with his son’s hesitancy.

“And I’d be away from Miss Anderson,” James finally said. “I don’t wish to be away from Miss Anderson, Father, I am very fond of her.”

Mr. Southall gave a great sigh and started to pace in front of his son. After a moment he stopped and took James gently by the shoulders.

“I understand, James. I truly do. But this opportunity is too great to squander. Does Rebecca feel as strongly about you as you do for her?” Mr. Southall already knew the answer to this but he wanted to make a point.

James stared down at his feet. “I believe so, sir,” he said softly.

“Well, then what are you worried about? You’re both too young to act on your feelings now anyway, and the experience you'll gain under General Nelson will place you in a better position to provide for Rebecca in the future. Surely, she will understand that."

"I suppose, Father, but it is still a great distance."

"Son, you won't be but twelve miles away, an easy ride. There will be plenty of opportunities to visit with each other."

James said nothing. He knew he could not go against his father's wishes. "Perhaps," he said finally, more to appease his father than to convey agreement.

"Let us then be open to the offer," urged Mr. Southall, forgetting that it was up to *James* to decide—not the both of them.

Two days later, when James, John, and Rebecca met at the brook, James shared the news of General Nelson's offer.

"That's grand, James!" exclaimed John, proud that such an important figure had selected his brother for consideration.

Rebecca's reaction was exactly what James had expected—and feared. She forced a smile. "Good for you, James. That is wonderful news." But she had trouble meeting his eyes, and her hands had entangled themselves in her hair, a clear sign that something was bothering her.

John saw that James and Rebecca needed some privacy, so he announced that he had forgotten to deliver a message from his father to Mr. Pitt, a merchant in town. He scrambled up the embankment and disappeared, leaving James and Rebecca alone.

"I'm sorry, Becca. I know you're upset," James whispered to her as he sat down beside her on a log.

"I'm fine, James," she said flatly. "Just surprised. It's an excellent opportunity for you and one you can't refuse."

"Father says the same thing, but… I don't want to be so far away."

"You won't be that far. My father and yours go to Yorktown often. Perhaps I can join them sometimes," she looked him in the eyes, "to visit you."

James nodded enthusiastically. "And I'm sure I can come home for Christmas and other times," he added. "Besides, it won't be forever. Just for a little while."

Rebecca reached for him and he hugged her tight, tears welling in their eyes.

General Nelson visited the Raleigh the following week and it was agreed that James would tutor four of the Nelson children. He would be treated as a family member, with a room of his own in the main house and meals with the family. He would also have use of a horse and be paid $240 a year.

The pay was significantly higher than what the Southalls had paid for their tutor just a few years earlier. This was not a testament to James and his ability, strong as it was, but rather the result of rampant price inflation that had ravaged Virginia's economy.

Paper money was largely to blame. All the states had printed paper money at the start of the war to pay their expenses; this was a common practice in times of war. And if done responsibly, paper money was an effective measure to cover war's high cost.

The paper money, however, needed to be backed up with something valuable, and the most valuable commodity in Virginia was tobacco. So, the government started collecting higher taxes paid in tobacco to match the value of the paper money it had printed.

This may have worked if the war had lasted just a year, but it went on and on and cost much more than anyone could have expected. Leaders in all the American states found they needed to raise taxes to pay for the war, but many—including Virginia's leaders—felt they had reached the limit on taxes.

Thus, they chose an easier solution: print more and more money *without* collecting more tobacco to pay for it. And so, by 1779 there was so much paper money circulating in Virginia that its value plummeted, causing prices to skyrocket. The price of tobacco in paper money in 1779 was eighteen times higher than it had been at the start of the war, and many other commodities and goods saw similar price increases. Items that cost two shillings before the war now cost thirty-six shillings in silver coins or more in paper money.

The inhabitants of Williamsburg tried to address this runaway inflation at a town meeting at the courthouse in mid-July. A list of prices for essential goods was agreed upon to combat price gouging and inflation. Wheat, flour, corn, oats, beef, bacon, mutton, lamb, butter, candles, and firewood were just some of the items included in the price fixing measure. Anyone caught charging more than the set price for an item on the list would be in violation of the agreement and be publicly criticized in the newspapers. It was hoped that such attention would convince people to follow the price guidelines.

A Committee of Inspection and Observation was formed to enforce the measure. Mr. Southall and Mr. Anderson both served on the committee and struggled all summer to enforce the new measures.

The measures proved to be largely ineffective because most merchants considered paper money worthless, and so they refused to sell their goods at the set paper money prices. Instead, they simply withheld these items for sale—claiming they didn't have them—which created a widespread shortage and resulted in an underground market where bartering and illegal sales in scarce silver and gold coins flourished.

Many buyers, in secret, offered double and triple the set prices in paper money for goods in the underground market, and merchants quickly realized they would be foolish to sell their goods out in the open at the set prices when so many people were willing to pay much more in secret for them. There was, unfortunately, little the Committee could do to prevent people from paying higher prices in paper money in the underground market. After all, it was their choice.

The summer of 1779 passed quickly for James and Rebecca. Rebecca let it be known to her many suitors that her affection was spoken for, and she spent as much time as she could with James, who visited her often at home.

"You know, people will say that you are courting me," she whispered to James one evening as they sat with Rebecca's parents and her little sister, Hope.

"They would be correct," James replied with a smile.

By the end of the summer, it was generally understood by all who knew them that James and Rebecca would someday marry. No one spoke of it openly—they were still too young for an engagement—but all agreed they made a good match and that in time, marriage would be in their future.

The Nelson House in Yorktown

Chapter Six

We Must Endure This Separation

1779

In late September, Mr. Southall transported James, along with a large trunk full of his clothing and books, to Yorktown in his wagon. James, who had said goodbye to Rebecca the prior evening, sat next to his father up front while John stretched out in the back and napped much of the way. Father and son said little on the journey, each consumed by their own thoughts. As they neared Yorktown, which the boys had visited on several occasions with their father, they were surprised by how much it had changed, or more correctly, declined.

Before the war, Yorktown had been a very busy and prosperous port town. Four years of war, however, had taken an economic toll.

Mr. Southall stopped the wagon just short of Mr. Nelson's house, an enormous, three-story brick building in the center of town. They climbed out of the wagon and John helped his brother carry the trunk up the steps to the front door. Mr. Southall knocked on the door and as they waited to be received, John looked at his brother.

John was sure James would excel as a tutor, but he also knew that while *he* might feel that way, James certainly did not. James was paler than usual and despite the chilly air, a thin layer of sweat had formed on his forehead. *Sick with worry,* thought John. The Nelson's were one of the most prominent families in York County, if not the entire region, and to be in General Nelson's fine home was surely intimidating. Wanting to ease his brother's nerves, John placed a steadying hand on his back. "I know you'll do fine brother," he whispered. "This is no different than another term at school, except *you* get to be the bully if you wish."

John felt James relax a bit under his touch, but the smile he gave John was anything but relaxed. It stretched tight across his face, clearly forced.

An enslaved woman opened the door to let the three in. They were greeted by General Nelson, who approached from a back room. "Welcome, welcome gentlemen. We are all so pleased you have decided to join us. Come in, please come in."

Mr. Southall and his sons bowed formally, which General Nelson returned. "Celia," General Nelson said to the enslaved woman, "fetch Benjamin and have him take Mr. Southall's trunk upstairs to his room."

Celia nodded and disappeared down the hall. General Nelson turned back to his guests with a smile. "Shall we withdraw to the parlor, gentlemen?"

As much as Mr. Southall wanted to socialize with General Nelson, he declined to stay. "I'm sorry, general. We haven't the time. I have several errands to run in town," he placed a hand on John's shoulder, "and we need to return before dark."

"I understand, sir," General Nelson replied. "Thank you for delivering your son to us."

"Of course, sir."

John glanced again at his brother. The nervous sweat had intensified and his posture seemed unnaturally straight. He stood so still that John was afraid he had stopped breathing. He cleared his throat in an attempt to get James's attention, but his brother refused to look at him.

"And you, sir," General Nelson said suddenly to John, "do you still have a taste for sweet bread?"

John flushed, embarrassed that General Nelson remembered the incident. "N-no, sir," he stammered.

"Colo—I mean General Washington fixed me of that long ago."

"Ah yes, I know the story well," the general chuckled before turning his attention back to Mr. Southall. "Will you at least take some refreshment?"

"We thank you again, sir, but we really haven't the time," Mr. Southall insisted.

General Nelson nodded, resolving to drop the matter. "Understood. I shall leave you to say goodbye and then see you out." General Nelson moved toward the front door, giving his guests some privacy.

Mr. Southall turned to James and extended his hand. "Do us proud, son," he said placing his left hand over his right as they shook.

"I'll do my best, sir," James replied, surprised by the emotion he sensed in his father. Mr. Southall glanced at John as if to say, "your turn," and then made his way toward the door to join General Nelson.

John stepped forward and said confidently, "You'll thrive here," but James gave him that same tight, uneasy smile.

"Brother!" John whispered, "You must relax! You are so nervous you appear sick. The Nelsons may send you back home with us, worried they'll catch something from you."

James turned even whiter. John couldn't help it, he burst out in laughter. "I'm sorry," he started. "But it is true. You look like a ghost." He wiped the sweat from James's brow and placed both hands on his brother's shoulders. "They would not have asked you here if they did not think you able, James. You can do this. Have confidence."

James finally met his brother's eyes. John had always been the more self-assured one, but he had never spoken to James in this way. It was as if their roles had reversed—John the elder brother and James the younger. James took a step back from his brother and took a deep breath. "Thank you," he began. "I guess I'm just worried because things will be very different from now on."

John shrugged. "Change can be good," he said. "Isn't that what we are fighting for? Change?"

James smiled. His brother was right. Being so far away from his family and Rebecca would be difficult, but this was a remarkable opportunity.

James offered his hand to his brother, which John clasped firmly. "Thank you, John." He pulled his brother in for a hug. "Watch after Becca for me," he said softly as they pulled apart.

John gave one final nod and then headed for the door, leaving James alone in the hallway.

James took another deep breath and gave each of his cheeks a hard squeeze—hoping to bring some color to his face so that he looked less like a ghost. He heard the mumblings of goodbyes and then heavy footsteps—General Nelson's. He wiped his brow and took another deep breath. *You can do this,* he thought.

"Well then, Mr. Southall, wel—" General Nelson paused, his brows furrowed. "Are you feeling all right? You look a bit flushed."

James's hands flew to his cheeks. "I feel quite well, sir. The wind was rather strong on the way here, and it is chillier than usual for this time of year."

General Nelson nodded, the tension melting from his face. "Indeed, it is, sir. Well, welcome again, Mr. Southall. We are so pleased to have you with us."

"It is my pleasure to serve."

General Nelson, who was a tall man similar in stature to General Washington, gestured toward the back of the house. "Let me show you our home, sir."

They stepped under the staircase and entered a back parlor. The room held two full bookcases along the wall with subjects ranging from philosophy and law to history and agriculture. In the center of the room was a large round table with several maps spread upon it. Six fine Windsor chairs were placed along the back wall, at rest, ready to be used.

"My library is at your disposal," said the general, "I hope you find it useful."

James's eyes grew wide as he admired the assorted titles. "It is a fine collection of books, sir." He felt his shoulders relax, the tension fade away. While this library was certainly fancier than anything he was used to, books had always been a grand comfort for James and he felt at ease in the room.

General Nelson smiled. "You may find this room useful for instruction as well," he said as he motioned for James to follow him.

When they re-entered the central passage, General Nelson gestured to a closed door across the hall. "That is my bedchamber," he said. "Mrs. Nelson has her own upstairs." He then led James to the dining room, the largest room in the house and very finely furnished.

As James stood in the doorway admiring the room, Mrs. Nelson descended the stairs. “Ah, Mrs. Nelson,” cried her husband, “allow me to introduce you to Mr. Southall.”

Mrs. Nelson curtsied. “Welcome to our home, Mr. Southall.”

James bowed low, his arm nearly sweeping the floor. “It is an honor to be here, Mrs. Nelson.”

“We are so pleased you have agreed to tutor the children,” said Mrs. Nelson. “My nephew William speaks very highly of you.”

James grinned. “And I hold Lieutenant Nelson in the highest regard.”

“Dear,” General Nelson said, “shall we gather the children in the parlor to meet their new tutor?”

“Indeed,” Mrs. Nelson nodded. “Kate!” she called out. A few seconds passed and a young enslaved woman descended the stairs and appeared at the doorway, awaiting directions. “Instruct the children to attend to us in the parlor,” Mrs. Nelson said. Kate curtsied and dashed back upstairs.

“Shall we proceed?” General Nelson said with a sweep of his hand toward the parlor.

Mrs. Nelson led the way and the Nelsons took seats on either side of the large fireplace, while James remained standing—hands folded in front of him so he would not be tempted to fiddle nervously with his fingers— facing the parlor's entrance.

The children arrived very orderly and as a group, the boys bowing and the girls curtsying as they entered.

Philip was the oldest at thirteen, followed by his brothers Francis, twelve, Hugh, eleven, and his sister Elizabeth, nine. They lined up side by side and stood facing James. Five-year-old Mary stood back a bit, clutching Kate's hand.

"Our two youngest, Lucy and Robert, remain upstairs with their nanny," said Mrs. Nelson.

"And of course, you know that our two oldest sons, William and Thomas, are at the college," added General Nelson. "Now, without further ado, may I present to you your young scholars, Philip, Francis, Hugh, and Elizabeth." The boys honored James with bows and Elizabeth curtsied. James bowed in return.

"Your lessons will begin tomorrow, children. Now off with you until dinner," said the general, waving his hand dismissively.

The boys bowed and Elizabeth curtsied to the Nelsons and James once more before quietly withdrawing from the parlor.

"Make yourself comfortable, Mr. Southall," General Nelson said, gesturing to a chair. "We wish to discuss the curriculum for the children."

James took a seat and a discussion of academic subjects ensued. It was agreed that Latin, Greek, and mathematics were crucial subjects for the boys. Elizabeth was to also learn some Latin and math, but reading and penmanship were to be a priority for her.

"Then it is agreed," said General Nelson. "Instruction shall begin tomorrow in my library after breakfast." He and his wife then shared their insight into each child's strengths and weaknesses, as well as their individual personalities. James did his best to commit each tidbit to memory, but as the conversation ran on, he found it increasingly difficult to remember all the information. Still, he was grateful for the Nelson's thorough description and felt much more comfortable than when he had first entered the home.

Finally, the Nelsons ended the conversation by thanking James once again for accepting the position.

General Nelson rose, prompting James to follow suit. The general called out for Celia, then said to James, "we have a bed chamber upstairs for your use and you are to dine with us every day."

By then Celia had emerged in the doorway. "Please show Mr. Southall to his bed chamber and help him get settled," General Nelson paused to look at a clock on the mantel. "Dinner will be in an hour. We will see you then." He then gestured toward the door and bowed slightly, prompting James to return the bow and head for the door.

James trailed Celia upstairs and thanked her for her help when they reached his bed chamber. He asked her to bring a wash basin with water and soap. *I must look more presentable for dinner,* he thought, *and not be so nervous.* There was no reason for such nervousness anyway, as the Nelson's seemed very grateful and pleased with him.

The children, however, might be another story. James plopped down on the bed and sighed. The children appeared polite and disciplined in the parlor, but that could very well be a façade. The Nelsons were a prominent family, and while James loved his family and was proud of all of his father's accomplishments, he knew that when it came to social standing, the Southalls were well below the

Nelsons. James worried the children would think him inferior and unworthy of their respect, just as some of the boys at the college had.

They will surely test me, perhaps at dinner, he thought, *so I must set the best impression possible for them*. Having the approval of General Nelson and his wife was only part of the battle—James also needed the acceptance of his pupils.

To his great relief, however, James discovered that General Nelson and his wife were firm disciplinarians who had raised very polite and obedient children. He would have no trouble from them.

James described his impression of his new students to Rebecca in his first letter, written two days after his arrival and only a day after his first lesson.

September 25, 1779

Dearest Rebecca,

I am well situated with General Nelson's family and have been accepted by all. My four scholars, three boys and a girl, range from nine to thirteen. They are all polite and respectful. Philip, the eldest, expects to attend the college next year, and this makes him especially earnest in his studies. His brothers, Francis and Hugh, also express an interest to learn, as does their sister Elizabeth. She reminds me of you at nine, responsible and eager to correct her older brothers when necessary.

The residence is the grandest I have ever been in, and I have a fine bed chamber upstairs. Dinner is a very pleasant affair with excellent conversation, and I dare say I will emerge from this experience better fed and more knowledgeable than when I entered it.

I do miss you, Becca. The thought that I shall see you over Christmas is my sole comfort. Until then, I pray that you and your family remain well.

I am, Ever Affectionately Yours,

James

Rebecca received the letter three days after it had been written. It was her very first letter and was delivered by Mr. Thomas Everard, the clerk of the court for York County, who traveled back and forth from Williamsburg to Yorktown regularly. She immediately penned a reply and delivered it to Mr. Everard the very next morning.

"I won't be returning to Yorktown for a few days," Mr. Everard informed her. "But I will gladly deliver it when I go."

Rebecca thanked him several times and then returned home. Her letter reached James four days later.

September 28, 1779

Dearest James,

I received your favor of the 25th and am delighted that your situation with the Nelsons is as pleasant as you say. I had full confidence you would excel as their tutor, and it appears that you are well on your way. Since your departure, I too have taken on some tutoring. My little scholar is none other than Hope. As she is only six years old, I'm sure I can handle the subject matter.

I earnestly hope that your time with the Nelsons continues to be enjoyable and useful, and that you can return home for Christmas.

The thought of John as my dance partner is terrifying, so please make arrangements to stay for the season as long as possible.

Until then, please continue to write and remain well.

Affectionately Yours,

Rebecca

Chapter Seven

Home for Christmas

1779

The letters that passed between James and Rebecca helped ease their separation, and the war had become an afterthought as they focused instead on their new responsibilities and their letters to one another. But the war with Great Britain continued, and in mid-November, troubling news from Savannah arrived.

For two years, Virginians had hoped that the alliance with France would produce victories on the battlefield, and in October of 1779, it appeared that a combined French and American army outside of Savannah, Georgia would finally be successful.

Alas, the British defenses of Savannah proved too strong to break, and the two allied armies that had attacked the British garrison there suffered tremendous casualties in a futile effort to storm the city. Hundreds of Continental Virginians had participated in the attack, and scores had been killed and wounded.

Two weeks after he'd learned of it in the newspapers, John was still upset about the crushing defeat. It was late November and John sat with Rebecca on the porch of the Raleigh, his head in his hands. "I just don't understand why we failed," he sighed. "The French navy had them cut off and trapped, *and* we outnumbered them with our troops and the French."

"Father says it was foolish to storm their lines," Rebecca said. "He says we should have kept to the siege until they surrendered."

John rolled his eyes. "Well, that's easy to say now," he growled.

Rebecca loathed speaking with John when he was in such a mood. He became irritatingly combative, and she had no desire to argue with him. She changed the subject to something cheerier—John's approaching birthday, just a month away. "Are you excited for your birthday?" she asked.

"Am I ever!" cried John.

Rebecca realized quickly that she had made a poor decision. Birthdays were, of course, a time of celebration and merriment, and she'd thought that steering the conversation in that direction would distract John from the negative news and lift his sour mood. It had done that, but not for the reasons she hoped.

John's next birthday would be his 16th, the age of eligibility for the militia, or worse—the Continental Army. And based on his response, Rebecca feared he would be off to war the very day of his birthday.

"You're not going to join the Continentals are you, John? You're going to stay here with the militia, right?"

John thought for a moment. In truth, he had always considered the Continentals. But he could tell by the way Rebecca was biting her lip that that was not what she wanted to hear. "I don't know, Becca," he said. "They are begging for Continental soldiers and I *can* join when I'm sixteen."

"That doesn't mean you should though! You should stay with the militia and get experience there. Remember what James said. It's not all glory, it's mostly marching and waiting around and shivering in the rain."

"I know, I know," said John. "I honestly haven't decided yet."

Rebecca scowled at him and John felt a flush of guilt. Now it was his turn to change the subject. "You know,

James turns seventeen next week," he said. "Has he written you lately?"

"He has. He continues to do well. Oh, and he's joined Captain Gibbon's company of *militia* in Yorktown."

John bit down a smile at Rebecca's emphasis of militia—he didn't want to go down that path again with her. John was willful and a good debater, but he knew Rebecca could be just as spirited. He did not want to fight with his dearest friend. "And what of Christmas?" he asked.

"He says he expects to be home the day before Christmas. He will be here until New Year's."

"Outstanding!" cried John. "You'll have a dance partner for Father's ball on the 28th. I'm spared!"

"I think you mean *I* am spared," Rebecca laughed.

Another month passed before James returned to Williamsburg. He arrived before dinner on Christmas Eve and found his mother waiting for him on the porch of the Raleigh.

He dismounted his horse, tied it to a post, and bowed to his mother, who descended the steps to hug her eldest child.

"Welcome home, James," she said warmly.

James tightened his arms around her. “It’s good to be home, Mother.”

Released from his mother’s embrace, he turned to unstrap his portmanteau—which contained his clothes and belongings— from the back of the horse. Suddenly, the front door burst open and Rebecca appeared. James had just enough time to drop his portmanteau and catch Rebecca, who had flown down the steps and into his arms.

“We missed you, James!” she said. “Welcome home!”

James was embarrassed by the attention and blushed considerably as he lowered Rebecca down. “W-what are you doing here?” he sputtered.

Rebecca’s hands flew to her hips. “Are you not happy to see me?” she pouted.

“Of course, I am,” he chuckled nervously. “I just didn’t expect to see you right this instant.”

“I invited the Andersons over for dinner,” Mrs. Southall said with a smile. “We’ve all been waiting for you. Shall we head in?”

The three entered the Raleigh and were met immediately by Mr. Southall and John. The other Southall siblings trailed slightly behind. “Welcome home, son,” Mr.

Southall said, offering his hand. "Is your horse tied up out front?"

"He is," James replied. "General Nelson offered me Spartan. He's a fine horse." James stepped toward John and hugged him, then mussed the hair of his brother William and hugged each of his other siblings. "It's good to be home."

"It's good to have *you* home," Rebecca corrected, appearing by his side.

There were only a few guests staying at the Raleigh, so the Southall's held their dinner in the Apollo Room. It was the first time the family ever had their own dinner there, and all their best dishware was used to mark the special occasion.

James and Rebecca sat next to each other at the table, joined by the rest of their family members. There was a lot of laughter among the siblings around the table, and the mood was light as everyone was pleased that James had returned.

"How do you find your situation there, James?" Mr. Anderson asked.

"Very pleasant, sir. The children are very well mannered and eager to learn, and General Nelson and his wife are most hospitable."

"And tutoring?" asked his father. "How do you like that?"

"I think it suits me, sir."

His father smiled. "Indeed, I think it does."

The conversation briefly shifted to the Christmas season—the fifth one with war—and then on to the war itself and its impact on Williamsburg.

Compared to the previous few years, 1779 had been uneventful—with the exception of events in Georgia. The disastrous allied attack upon Savannah in October had left the British securely in control of Georgia. They also appeared secure in New York City, safe on Manhattan Island protected by the powerful British navy. General Washington and his army remained nearby, ready to strike if the British ventured out of the city, but General Henry Clinton, the overall British commander in America, showed little inclination to do so. As a result, a stalemate had developed in New York.

There was one impending development in Virginia, however, that promised significant change for the residents of Williamsburg, and John brought up the issue; the planned move of the capital from Williamsburg to Richmond.

Despite the General Assembly's vote in May to move the capital from Williamsburg, the Southalls and Andersons—along with most of Williamsburg—had hoped all year that the legislators would reconsider and rescind their decision. Months had passed without any action, however, and the reality of a move was becoming apparent.

"They're really going to do it, aren't they? They're going to move the government," John murmured.

Mr. Southall and Mr. Anderson frowned, but both gave John a slight, curt nod.

"I still can't believe that Richmond will suffice as a capital," complained Mr. Southall. "It's too small."

"I don't know where the government is going to find the resources to pay for the move," added Mr. Anderson. "Their paper notes are almost worthless as it is."

James had not given the move much thought—he had been too busy adjusting to his new position with the Nelsons. But now he realized that the move was indeed going to happen, and that Williamsburg would be gravely impacted.

"How will all of the taverns in town survive?" he asked before grasping the answer himself. *My God,* he thought with a start, *they won't.*

There was an uncomfortable silence for a moment, until Mrs. Southall cleared her throat. "We haven't time to worry about such things. We have a ball to plan for. It's in three days' time!"

"Indeed, we do," agreed Mr. Southall, happy for the change in topic.

The discussion of the upcoming ball became the focus of conversation and lasted well past dinner.

When the clock chimed six, Mr. Southall asked if anyone wanted to play a game of Whist or dice.

"I'm afraid we must be going," responded Mr. Anderson. "The life of a tavernkeeper, you know."

The Southalls smiled and nodded in understanding.

"May I stay?" Rebecca asked her parents as they got up to leave.

"If it is agreeable to Mrs. Southall," replied Rebecca's mother.

“Certainly, dear,” Mrs. Southall smiled. “Stay as long as you wish.”

Mr. Southall clapped his hands. “Let us walk you out and reconvene in the Daphne Room,” he announced. The Daphne room was a private club room situated between the Apollo Room and the Billard Room at the end of the tavern. Mr. Southall turned to Tom, one of his enslaved people who had waited on them all evening. “Start a fire in the Daphne Room and let this one burn down; we are finished here,” he said.

Mr. Southall and John paired up against James and Rebecca for the first few rounds of Whist, while Mrs. Southall tended to the younger children, who needed to be put to bed. When she returned, John dutifully rose and offered her his seat, which she accepted. John sat off to the side at a small table and played a game of Shut the Box by himself.

After just three rounds of cards, however, Mrs. Southall yawned loudly and unexpectedly. “My goodness, forgive me,” she said. “It’s been a long day. Perhaps we should turn in, dear.”

Mr. Southall nodded, rising from his chair. “Rebecca, be sure to thank your family for joining us this evening. It was a pleasure.”

Rebecca curtsied. “Thank you again for inviting us. It was lovely.”

“May we remain?” John cut in, knowing that Rebecca could not ask for more time herself, and that James likely would be too shy to do so. “I’m feeling lucky with the dice now,” he lied.

“Of course,” said Mrs. Southall, “but no betting.”

John brought the dice game to the card table and the three friends played multiple rounds of Shut the Box, reveling in each other’s company after James’s long absence. Many things had changed for the friends over the years—some for the better, Rebecca and James likely thought—but in this moment all three felt as if they had been transported back to simpler times, back to when they thought that the war would end quickly and in victory.

By ten o’ clock, despite her best efforts, it was Rebecca’s turn to yawn loudly.

“Shall I walk you home?” James asked.

“I think perhaps it is time,” responded Rebecca as she slowly rose from the table.

"I'm not leaving until I shut the box," cried John, rolling the dice over and over again in search of the right combination of rolls to win the game.

Rebecca laughed. "Well, good luck, John, and good night." She curtsied to John and reached for James's hand. John, who was focused on his next roll of the dice, gave Rebecca only a hurried nod and a wave.

Although she was tired, Rebecca insisted that they take their usual route via the Capitol back to her house. As they walked arm in arm down Duke of Gloucester Street, she rested her head on James's shoulder. The two had been eager for some time alone when the evening had started, but now found themselves unable to speak.

When they reached the capitol, however, Rebecca stopped walking. "What will become of it?" she asked, staring at its large red bricks.

"I don't know. It's a fine building though. Seems a shame to abandon it."

They continued along the circle and headed back up the street to Rebecca's house. The city was dark and quiet, not typical for the capital, and both wondered if this was a sign of things to come for Williamsburg.

When they reached Rebecca's steps, she took hold of James's hands. "It was a wonderful evening, James. Please thank your parents for inviting us."

"I hope it's the first of many such dinners."

They embraced and Rebecca whispered, "Good night, James. It's so nice to have you back." She kissed him good night and ascended the stairs, stopping briefly at the front door. She whirled around quickly and curtsied. "Good evening Mr. Southall," she said playfully, her voice mockingly formal.

James smiled and bowed formally in response to play along. Rebecca gave one last laugh and then shut the door behind her, leaving James smiling from ear to ear.

Over the next few days, the young couple spent as much time as they could with each other, sometimes at Rebecca's house and sometimes at his. John often joined them, but not always. He was aware that they desired some time to themselves.

On the day of the Southall's ball, it had started snowing and continued into the evening. This did not deter guests from attending, however. The opportunity to dance drew people to the Raleigh Tavern like moths to a flame.

The Southalls did their best to provide an assortment of refreshments, but four and a half years of war had disrupted the economy so much that many of the usual Christmas delicacies were difficult or impossible to get. The dancing went on, however, and that is what mattered most to James and Rebecca.

Unlike their first ball in the Capitol two years earlier, where James had contended with multiple young men for Rebecca's attention, this year he managed to secure nearly every dance with her. They both danced with their parents as well, of course—Rebecca with her father twice and James once with his mother—but the rest of the dances that evening were reserved for each other.

John stood off to the side, happy for his brother and his friend. *They look good together,* he thought. *James is a lucky man.*

Most at the dance agreed, including General and Mrs. Nelson, who commented on what a fine pair the two made.

"Thank you, sir," replied James with a bow, Rebecca curtsying at the same time to show her thanks. "And the children," James continued, "they are well?"

"Yes, yes, they are fine. They send their regards. I told them you would return after Twelfth Night, if that is agreeable to you, of course."

"Indeed, it is," said James, realizing with joy that his break had just been extended by nearly a week.

The ball continued well past midnight and by the end, Rebecca protested that she was too tired to take their normal, roundabout way home, so they crossed the street and proceeded directly to her house. It was cold, and the snow had turned to freezing pellets, so they remained at the foot of her steps only long enough for James to tell her that his visit had been extended.

"That's wonderful, James," Rebecca squealed, stepping forward to hug him. "The perfect gift!"

"I wish I could stay even longer," he whispered in her ear.

Rebecca hugged James a little tighter in response. But the biting wind and freezing rain stung their ears and soon separated them. "I hate to say goodbye," James said, "but you must get inside before you catch cold." He took Rebecca's hand and walked her up the steps to the front door where he said good night with a kiss.

The next day was John's 16th birthday, and James and Rebecca strove to make the day all about him.

Williamsburg was covered with snow, coated with a thin glaze of ice, and although they were exhausted from the night before, the three friends met in the morning and walked about town to enjoy the view.

"So now that you are finally sixteen, what are your intentions?" James asked.

"Oh, I don't know," John mumbled. "I'm still thinking."

Rebecca clapped John on the back in approval. "Good! Don't make any hasty decisions."

"No need to make any rash decisions now, in the winter," John chuckled. "The armies are all in winter quarters, so even if I did join, I'd just be stuck in camp. I can make a decision in the spring."

"Indeed," said James, "that is well thought. You always hear of men clamoring for furloughs to go home during the winter. No sense to rush off to camp when everyone else wants to leave."

Rebecca was relieved that John had decided to wait, but she still worried that he would eventually join the Continentals. If he did, his chances for harm would skyrocket compared to the militia, and the thought made her sick to her stomach. Still, she kept her thoughts to herself as the brothers chatted more about military service.

The end of the Christmas season, which ended the twelfth night after Christmas, came all too quickly for James and Rebecca, and James returned to Yorktown the following day.

Two weeks after his return, however, James received a letter from Rebecca with shocking news. Her father had decided to give up the lease on the Williamsburg tavern and move the family to Richmond to run a tavern in the new capital.

“We are to leave in March,” she wrote. “Father says there is no future for the tavern business in Williamsburg now that the government is leaving.”

James was crushed. Williamsburg was less than a half day’s ride from Yorktown, some twelve miles away. Richmond, however, was over sixty miles—two full days by horse—away.

James understood Mr. Anderson’s decision; he had a family to provide for after all and so had to move wherever there was business, but the thought of being so far away from Rebecca was unbearable. Yet, there was nothing to be done about it. The decision had been made.

"We must endure this separation, Becca," he urged in his next letter. "It will only be for a short while."

Chapter Eight

John Joins the Continentals

1780

John was stunned when he learned that the Andersons were moving to Richmond, but he had his own news that was equally significant—he had decided to enlist with the Virginia Continentals for eighteen months. He had kept the decision to himself for over a month, but finally resolved to reveal it to Rebecca in late February at their favorite spot, the brook.

When he arrived to share the news, Rebecca was already there, waiting for him. She had a forlorn look on her face, almost as if she knew what was coming and this caused John to hesitate.

"Well," she started, "out with it then."

John hung his head, his voice barely a whisper. "I am going to enlist with the Virginia Continentals."

Rebecca had suspected all along that he would do so, so her reaction was muted. She gave a stiff nod, her gaze firmly on the rushing water, refusing to meet John's eyes.

John sat down beside her. "I only signed up for eighteen months, Becca," he said sheepishly. "Not for the duration of the war like some. I passed up a bounty of $750 and one hundred acres of land because I knew you'd be furious if I joined for the duration."

"Oh, so it is to be just a year and a half of your life in danger," she said flatly. "No harm can come to you in such a short amount of time," she cracked sarcastically." She did not want to fight with John, but his decision upset her. *The militia is so much safer you damned fool,* she thought. *Why couldn't you be satisfied with the militia like James?*

John moved closer to Rebecca but was unsure what to say. Every topic he conjured up seemed to run the risk of further upsetting her.

Rebecca hugged her knees to her chest and nestled her forehead into the small crook. "We're all scattering now," she sighed, "going our separate ways. Curse this war!"

John put his arm around her. "I'm sorry, Becca. But I've got to do this. I couldn't live with myself if I didn't enlist. I've got to do my part."

Rebecca lifted her head from its hiding place and swiped away her tears. "I understand, John. I truly do. Just…" she paused, finally looking him in the eyes.

"Promise me you'll be careful. That you won't do anything too rash."

John squeezed her shoulders tight. "I promise. Nothing *too* rash."

Rebecca sighed as she laid her head on his shoulder. "When do you leave?"

"Sometime next week. A lieutenant is coming to take me and several others to Petersburg where the Continentals are encamped. I guess we'll get sorted out there."

She lifted her head off his shoulder, her face deadly serious as she stared at him. "Just be careful, John. *Please* be careful."

Lieutenant Joseph Wilson arrived late in the afternoon less than a week later and stayed overnight at the Raleigh.

"We're to leave in the morning, Mr. Southall," he informed the young recruit, "so you best have your affairs in order."

John's father provided his son with a pack and John filled it with two shirts, two pairs of stockings, a linen weskit, a pair of overalls, a pair of breeches, a wool blanket, a large oil cloth to protect from the rain, a wooden bowl, a tin cup, a pewter spoon and fork, a toothbrush, a chunk of soap, a horn comb, a sewing kit with spare buttons, and a bound journal with two pencils. There was room for little else in the pack, but Mrs. Southall had miraculously managed to squeeze in some dried fruit—John's favorite.

At the end of dinner, John excused himself and went across the street to say goodbye to Rebecca.

"Hello, John," Mr. Anderson said when John entered the central passage. "I expect I know why you're here. Let me find Rebecca for you."

Mr. Anderson disappeared to the back of the tavern where their private quarters were. As he waited, Mrs. Anderson emerged and approached John, her brows knitted together in concern.

"So, I suppose the time has come to say goodbye," she sighed as she took hold of his hands. "You are a dear boy, John. Please be careful."

"I will, ma'am."

Finally, Rebecca entered the passage, her eyes misty and the skin around them red. Mrs. Anderson gestured toward the unoccupied club room, directing the two in there for privacy.

"Sit," Rebecca said softly as she motioned to the nearby chairs. "I have a gift for you." Her hand slipped into her pocket and reemerged grasping a pair of fingerless wool gloves. She had spent the past week frantically knitting them, worried she would not finish in time. "I thought these might be useful for you," she said as she settled into the chair across from him.

John smiled and kissed Rebecca on the cheek. "Thank you, Becca. Always so thoughtful." He slipped one of the gloves onto his hand and grinned as he held it up for Rebecca to admire. "Perfect fit."

Rebecca nodded, but said nothing. John lowered his hand and reached for hers. "Becca," he said quietly, "may I, may I have a lock of your hair? As a keepsake?"

Rebecca laughed in surprise. "Really?"

John's cheeks started to redden. "Well, I mean, I—"

Rebecca laughed again, rising from her chair. "Of course you can, John," she said. "But only if I can have a lock of yours."

John smiled. "Of course."

Rebecca retrieved a pair of scissors and two thin blue ribbons from the back room. Each then snipped a piece of hair from the other and Rebecca tied them up nicely. She walked to the marble fireplace mantle where an empty brass snuff box had been sitting for weeks. She placed her lock of hair inside the box, turned back to John, and gave her most formal curtsy. “For you, sir,” she said with mock gravity.

John smiled and returned the favor with his own deeply formal bow. “Apologies,” he said as he straightened and held the lock of hair out to her. “I do not have a box for yours.”

Rebecca accepted the lock gingerly, tucking it into her pocket with care. “I will keep it with me always,” she said softly.

“As will I,” John smiled.

Rebecca threw her arms around her friend, surprising John with her strength. “You be careful, John Southall,” she said into his chest. “You just be careful.”

John felt her tears seep through his shirt, causing tears of his own to well. He blinked them away and smoothed Rebecca’s hair, afraid if he spoke his voice would betray him.

Suddenly, Rebecca’s parents appeared in the doorway, causing the two to split. Rebecca rubbed at her eyes, embarrassed.

“He’ll be fine dear,” Mr. Anderson assured his daughter. “He’s a clever lad.”

Rebecca smiled, tears running down her cheeks and thought, *lad, yes, he's just a lad. He shouldn't be going*. But she knew there was nothing that would stop him.

"God keep you, son," said Mrs. Anderson as John made his way toward the door.

"Thank you, ma'am," replied John. "Good luck in Richmond."

He stepped onto the porch, followed by Rebecca.

"I will write to you. So, you better answer my letters," she called out as he descended the stairs.

"I will, I will," he chuckled as he walked away into the street. He didn't want Rebecca and her parents to see the tears that had finally freed themselves from his eyes, but the Andersons knew. When he reached the other side of the street he turned back and waved a final time to his best friend.

I shall miss her, he thought as he watched Rebecca wave back. He gave her one last smile and then turned, wiping his tearstained cheeks, and went inside the Raleigh.

Lieutenant Wilson had no time for long goodbyes the next morning as he wished to reach New Kent Courthouse—thirty miles away—by dinner. Seven recruits joined John on the porch of the Raleigh at 8 a.m. They had already bid goodbye to their families and had met at the Raleigh as instructed. The Southalls were all gathered around John on the porch, while Lieutenant Wilson and the recruits waited in the street.

Mr. Southall stood stiffly on the porch, no noticeable emotion on his face. “Make us proud, son,” is all he said as he extended his hand.

John’s mother showed far less restraint. She dabbed tears from her eyes and wrapped John in her arms tightly. “Please be careful, my son,” she choked out between sobs. “And write to us when you can.”

John promised to do so, then gave hugs to his siblings and walked down the stairs. Lieutenant Wilson sat upon a horse and two of the other recruits sat in the wagon, which was driven by a sergeant. The wagon was full of linen cloth woven in Williamsburg, shoes made in town, and sacks of corn meal.

“Throw your pack in the back with the others, Mr. Southall,” instructed Lieutenant Wilson. “We can’t overload the wagon, so you need to walk with the others. But you’ll get your turn in the wagon soon enough.”

The lieutenant gestured to the sergeant to proceed and the small party started its journey. Rebecca and her family stood on their porch and waved as they passed. John gave a short wave back, but then snapped his head forward, not wishing to reveal the sadness he felt to his new comrades.

John was the only recruit from the city itself. The others had been raised on the outskirts of town. They were all older than he was, though not by much, and John recognized a couple of them, but only vaguely.

John and the others on foot followed alongside the wagon, three on one side and two on the other. Lieutenant Wilson led the party on horseback. Everyone was silent until they passed the college and John finally decided to introduce himself to the two recruits walking with him.

He tapped the tall lanky fellow in front of him on the shoulder. "I'm John Southall, what's your name?"

"Pleased to meet you, Mr. Southall," he replied. "I'm William McLaughlin, and that there is Simon Pagett," he pointed to the person in front of him.

Simon just waved a quick acknowledgment over his shoulder and kept walking.

John wanted to converse, but he was concerned he'd get in trouble so he said nothing else until they stopped to rest.

After the first stop, the two men who walked opposite John exchanged places with the men in the wagon. John's feet throbbed and he glanced at the men in the wagon several times with envy.

After another stop to rest, however, the lieutenant instructed John and the other two men with him to ride in the wagon. Simon Paget sat up with the sergeant while John and William squeezed in right behind them. John gave a sigh of relief as he settled in.

"So, your father is Captain Southall?" William asked, his hands busy rubbing the soles of his feet. "How old are you anyway?"

"Just a few months past sixteen," said John.

William frowned. "What are you doing in the Continentals then? You should have stayed with the militia. They couldn't draft you for two more years."

John was surprised at the question—he'd thought all young men would be as eager as he was to fight. "I wanted to do my part," he said. "And I figured the Continentals needed me the most."

William nodded, but his expression of confusion remained. Simon, who was also listening, shook his head in disbelief.

"How long have you been with the army, sergeant?" asked John, wanting to take the attention off himself.

"Too long," barked the sergeant with a laugh. "This is my second enlistment. I signed up for two years in '76 and re-enlisted at Valley Forge for three more."

John's eyes widened. "You were at Valley Forge?"

"For a spell. They let me come home on furlough for most of it in return for re-enlisting."

"So, that means you were at Monmouth?" John continued.

The sergeant nodded. "Indeed, I was. And Brandywine, Germantown, Whitemarsh, and Stony Point, too."

John was impressed. "What's your name, sergeant?"

"Baley," he said. "And you' re Captain Southall's son, are you not? What's your name, lad?"

"John, sir. Pleased to meet you."

The sergeant only nodded in response; eyes focused on the horses pulling the wagon.

"How much further do we have, sergeant?" Simon asked.

"We're not even halfway there," Sergeant Baley chuckled. "Everyone will rotate through twice more before we reach the courthouse."

Just as Sergeant Baley predicted, each recruit had more walking to do and two more rides in the wagon before they reached the courthouse in New Kent County.

Lieutenant Wilson had made arrangements to stay in the tavern across from the courthouse, but the recruits were to sleep on the floor of the courthouse with Sergeant Baley.

"Make yourselves comfortable," said the sergeant as he unloaded his pack and spread his blanket on the floor. "We'll dine at the tavern later."

Although Lieutenant Wilson had failed to secure beds for his recruits, he did secure dinner at the tavern—which he paid for with Continental currency. He did not eat with the men, however—that was left to Sergeant Baley. Lieutenant Wilson dined in a private club room with several gentlemen of the county instead.

It was nearly dark when John and the others finished dinner. They returned to the courthouse and prepared for bed. *This isn't so bad,* thought John as he lay staring at the ceiling. *I can handle this.*

The next morning, five other recruits joined their party and they were off before 7:30 a.m.

"I am determined to reach Petersburg, sergeant," announced Lieutenant Wilson as they began the journey.

"How far is that?" asked John, who was standing next to Sergeant Baley, near the front of the wagon.

"About twenty-five miles," Sergeant Baley said matter-of-factly.

The second day was much like the first, with no real opportunity to converse except in the wagon. The additional recruits meant more walking for everyone, and by the time they reached Petersburg in the late afternoon, John could feel the effect on his feet.

These are the blisters James warned me about, thought John as his feet burned with pain. Fortunately for everyone, there would be no marching tomorrow—they had finally reached the Continental camp.

When they arrived, they found that Colonel Abraham Buford, the commander of the camp, was away in search of clothing and other supplies for the men. General William Woodford and the bulk of the Virginia Continental line from the main army were expected to arrive at any moment. Three months earlier, General Washington ordered all the Virginia Continentals with the main armyto march to South Carolina to reinforce General Benjamin Lincoln in Charleston. General Woodford commanded this force of several thousand Virginians, but his march south from New Jersey during the winter was long and difficult. His last report placed him in Fredericksburg with a much-diminished force—reduced by desertion, illness, fatigue, and the expiration of many enlistments.

Colonel Buford, a veteran of the now defunct 15th Virginia Regiment, had been in Virginia for most of the previous year, struggling to recruit and outfit the last of three Virginia detachments General Washington had ordered to South Carolina in the summer of 1779. Two of those detachments had marched south and fought at Savannah in October, but Buford's detachment was ill supplied with clothing—the men largely dressed in rags and unable to take the field. So, Buford remained in Petersburg and pressed Governor Jefferson to supply his men with clothing. He'd hoped to march south with General Woodford when he arrived, but as that time drew closer, he found most of his men were still inadequately clad.

John was not prepared for what he saw at the camp. He described his journey and the camp to Rebecca in his first letter to her.

March 3, 1780

Dear Becca,

I arrived in camp here in Petersburg yesterday afternoon, after two long days of walking alongside the wagon you saw when we left. I am told we traveled over fifty miles, and those blisters that James described on his march to Smithfield last year found their way to my feet. None of us walked the entire way, we each took turns riding in the wagon, but only for an hour or so, and then it was back to walking for most of the journey.

The camp here in Petersburg is in disarray and the condition of the men appalling. Many are quite naked, with only thin shirts and ragged overalls to wear. No one seems to have a coat, so they wrap themselves up in blankets for warmth. Not everyone has a blanket, however, and it would make you blush to see the condition of many of the men.

I am told we won't march until the men are properly clothed. The linen we brought should help toward that end, but I doubt it will be enough.

Our rations are adequate, as is our shelter, although I was much more comfortable at home. Nevertheless, I am determined to do my part and have no regrets about being here.

I expect you will be moving to Richmond soon. You must write to me as soon as you settle in to tell me about your new place and the town. I've never been there, but understand it is small and situated along the river.

Please give my best wishes to your parents as well as mine, if you get the chance. I expect to write to them, as well as James, soon.

I await your reply. Until then,

I remain, your ever Affectionate Friend,

John

Chapter Nine

Goodbye

1780

James returned home from Yorktown the day before the Andersons left for Richmond. The Southalls had the Andersons over for dinner—this time in a club room because guests were gaming in the Apollo Room. It was a pleasant, yet somber dinner, and when the Andersons left to return home, Rebecca stayed with James on the porch of the Raleigh.

It was a chilly night, but they nestled close together on a bench.

"How long did your father say it will take to get to Richmond?" James asked.

"He wants to make it in two days. We're staying at a tavern in New Kent Courthouse tomorrow night. He wrote and reserved a room two weeks ago."

"It's about fifty miles to Richmond, and New Kent Courthouse is about half that, so you shouldn't have any trouble getting to either place before dinner."

“I’m just glad I don’t have to walk any of it like John. Father has already moved most of our belongings and our people there, so we get to ride the whole way to Richmond in the wagon.”

“What has he said about the place you’re moving into?”

“He said it’s smaller than our current tavern, but it’s close to the courthouse, so he expects a lot of business.”

James smiled slightly. “Well, I am happy for him of course,” he said softly.

They chatted a bit longer in the cold before finally standing to take their last roundabout walk to Rebecca’s home. When they reached the former Capitol, empty and dark, they paused and thought of their first ball there.

“Do you think it will ever see another ball?” asked Rebecca wistfully.

“I doubt it,” James replied. “Everything will be different here.”

“I wish it wasn’t so,” Rebecca sighed. “It makes me sad to think of it.”

“Me too,” said James, “but there is nothing to be done about it.”

They continued around the circle and soon reached Rebecca's steps, where they stopped and gazed at each other. The air felt heavy, stifling even, despite the season.

"Write to me often," Rebecca said as she stepped into James's arms.

"I will, I will." James rested his chin on Rebecca's head. "But it won't be long. General Nelson has promised me some time off this summer, and I plan to spend it all in Richmond. I'll be a guest at your tavern and you can serve me," he said playfully.

They both laughed at the thought and then kissed goodnight.

"I'll see you off in the morning," James whispered as they hugged one last time. Then he offered his arm, walked her up the steps, and opened the front door for her.

"Goodnight, Becca. I love you."

"I love you too, James," she replied, bestowing a tender kiss on his cheek.

James woke with a start before dawn the next morning and dressed quickly. He sat staring out the dining room window at the Anderson's tavern, waiting for a sign that they were up and about. Mr. Anderson had closed the tavern two weeks earlier, using the time to transport most of their belongings to Richmond. They had just a half wagon load left to move, and as the first light of dawn appeared, James noticed Mr. Anderson and one of his enslaved men appear with a horse and wagon at the front of the tavern.

James sprang up, dashing out the front door and across the street. "Good morning, Mr. Anderson," he said as he approached. "May I help you load the wagon?"

"No need for that, James," Mr. Anderson said. "Why don't you go inside and see how Rebecca is coming along?"

James entered the front door and announced himself. Rebecca peeked out the doorway of the back room and smiled. "Just a minute," she said. She ducked back in the room, adjusted her clothing, and dashed back to the central passage where James was waiting.

"Couldn't sleep either?" she asked.

James nodded. "I've been up for a while waiting for you." There was an awkward pause, both unsure of what to say. James felt an overwhelming pressure to busy himself, lest his emotions get the best of him. "Is there anything I can help you with?" he asked.

"Can you carry my bedding out to the wagon?"

“Certainly.” James walked toward the back room, knocking twice before he entered to find Mrs. Anderson tending to Hope, who was still half asleep.

“Good morning, Mrs. Anderson, Hope,” he said as he scooped up Rebecca’s stuffed tick, blankets and pillow.

Hope only yawned in response. But Mrs. Anderson smiled. “Good morning, James,” she said. “Thank you for the help.”

James nodded and headed back out the door with Rebecca’s bedding. Rebecca followed him out the front door to the wagon.

“How is your mother coming along?” Mr. Anderson asked Rebecca.

“Fine. She’s almost done helping Hope get ready.”

“Well then, put your things aboard and say your goodbyes,” Mr. Anderson said as he headed inside the tavern to help his wife.

Rebecca tossed a bag with her clothing into the wagon and looked sadly at James. The two embraced one last time, holding each other until the Andersons reappeared from the tavern. Then James lifted Rebecca up into the wagon.

Mrs. Anderson led Hope to the wagon and James lifted her in as well, then helped Mrs. Anderson up onto the front seat. Mr. Anderson tossed the last of their things in the back, returned to the front door, locked it, and then returned to the wagon. He placed his hand on James's shoulder and squeezed. "Thank you for caring for Rebecca, son. I know this separation will be hard, but you two will overcome it soon enough. Give this key to your father and thank him and your mother for their kindness. We'll expect to see you in Richmond sometime soon."

James nodded and watched as Mr. Anderson climbed aboard the wagon and took the reins. "You two can ride in the back," Mr. Anderson said, turning to William and Jane, the last of his enslaved people in Williamsburg. "But when we reach a hill, you need to get out and walk to spare the horse." He faced forward and said to the horse, "Let's go," flicking the reins.

James reached out and took Rebecca's hand. Tears ran down both of their faces as the wagon began to move.

"I will see you soon," he said solemnly, walking with the wagon, still holding her hand. "I will see you soon."

Rebecca smiled but said nothing. Her words had dried and lodged themselves in her throat.

As the wagon picked up speed, James let go with a heavy sadness. He stood and watched the wagon slowly make its way down Duke of Gloucester Street toward the college and ultimately, Richmond. He swiped at his eyes, trying to clear the tears. *It won't be that long,* he thought. *It won't.*

James returned to General Nelson's home that same day, desperate for a distraction from his sadness.

The Andersons reached Richmond at the end of the second day of their journey. Rebecca was surprised at how small the new tavern was. Her father, however, was confident that it would do very well.

"I expect that we will all be very busy for some time," predicted Mr. Anderson, "too busy to dwell on sad things. Let us get to work, I want to open by the end of the week."

In Petersburg, John thought of Rebecca and her move to Richmond and knew that James was likely devastated by it, but had faith that the two would survive the separation.

Meanwhile, General Woodford had arrived from New Jersey on March 6th—the same day the Anderson's started out for Richmond—with just over seven hundred men. The encampment in Petersburg hummed with activity, despite the unexpectedly small number of troops with Woodford.

"I thought he had three thousand men with him," John said to Sergeant Baley on the evening of their arrival.

Sergeant Baley shrugged. "He probably did. This is what happens on long marches. Men get left behind or sneak away."

"Yes, but there aren't even a thousand men with him now," noted John. "Is it possible that he lost two thousand men on the march?"

"Sure, it's possible. You should have seen how many we lost in '76 marching from New York to the Delaware River. And that was under General Washington himself."

Wanting to abandon General Woodford I could understand, but General Washington? John thought, flabbergasted. *Though I suppose if even the great General Washington struggled to retain men, General Woodford losing two thousand isn't all that surprising.*

John was not fond of General Woodford. He knew him from his visits to the Raleigh tavern years earlier and found him arrogant. But beyond that, John disliked Woodford because of the disrespect he had shown Patrick Henry back in 1775, when Henry and Woodford commanded Virginia's two original regiments of regulars.

He abused Colonel Henry out of jealousy, thought John, *and he was a petty man for doing so. He's lucky to still have as many men as he does.*

General Woodford and his reduced force of seven hundred and thirty-seven men remained in Petersburg for just two days. A letter had arrived from General Benjamin Lincoln, commander of the American Southern army posted in Charleston, South Carolina, urging Woodford to hurry to Charleston as quickly as possible. A large British fleet and enormous army of eight thousand troops had arrived in South Carolina from New York, and General Lincoln needed reinforcements to defend Charleston.

John did not march south with General Woodford on March 8th, however. He remained behind with Colonel Buford's detachment—some four hundred men—most of whom were still too inadequately clothed to march.

Colonel Buford was often away from camp working mightily to remedy the situation, and by the end of March he had obtained enough clothing and supplies to lead the last detachment of Virginia Continentals still in the state to Charleston. John, who was one of the better outfitted men in the detachment, was glad to be on the move. *This is it,* he thought excitedly. *I'm off to war.*

Map of the Carolinas

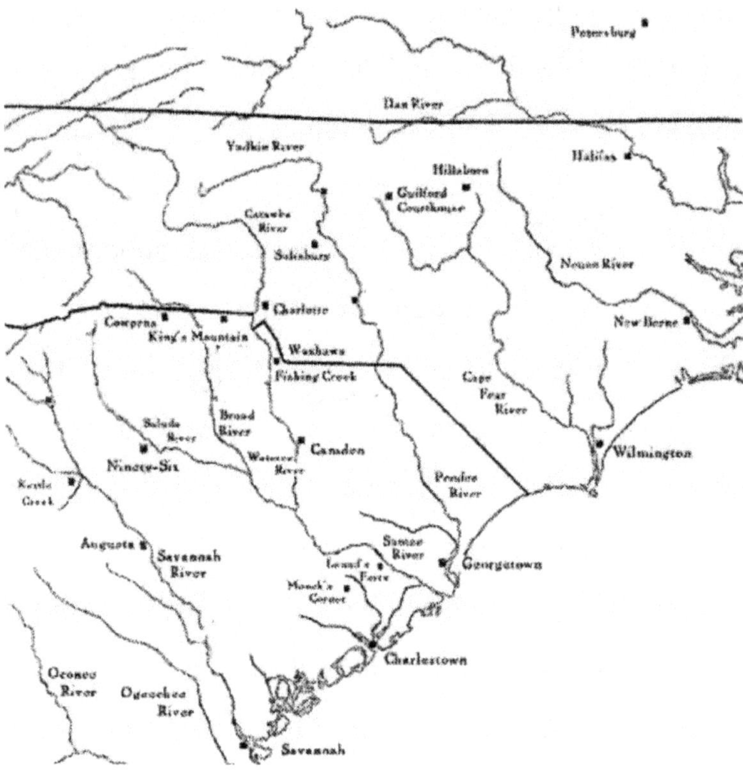

Chapter Ten

Battle of Waxhaws

May 1780

Colonel Buford's detachment was divided into eight companies of approximately forty-five men, each commanded by a captain, two lieutenants and three sergeants. John served in Captain Adam Wallace's company. Captain Wallace was a veteran officer from Frederick County, and John was told by several experienced soldiers that he was fortunate to be under his command. The company was even more fortunate to have experienced lieutenants and sergeants, one of whom ended up taking John under his wing.

"So, you're Captain Southall's boy, are you?" Sergeant John Ballard asked when they first met in camp.

"Yes, sir," replied John.

"Are you his oldest?"

"No, sir. That would be my brother James."

"Well, I'm Sergeant Ballard. I've been to your father's tavern many times, but not for some time. I do recall a youngster or two about, would one of them have been you?"

"Probably, sir. My brother was likely away at school."

"Hmmm." Sergeant Ballard paused as he looked John up and down. John was tall and lean, but his face still had that youthful glow that only children seem to have. "How old are you?"

John straightened, thrusting his shoulders back and holding his head up ever so slightly. "Sixteen and a half," he said gruffly.

Sergeant Ballard laughed and shook his head. "Well, I'll be sure to keep my eye on *you,* lad. That's mighty young for this company."

John flushed in embarrassment. He knew he was young, but despite his boyish appearance, he was not a child. *I'll show him,* he thought. *I was meant to be a soldier*. Still, as he looked around the camp, he had to admit that Sergeant Ballard was right. There were a lot of veteran soldiers in Captain Wallace's company, including Sergeant Baley and Lieutenant Wilson, who had brought John to Petersburg several weeks earlier. Among them all, John was clearly the youngest and least experienced.

John's inexperience with army life frequently displayed itself, much to his irritation and the amusement of the veterans. John knew the basics: standing in formation, marching, handling his musket, etc. All of those things were easy, given he had practiced them with his father's militia company. But he struggled with the daily skills of a soldier.

John didn't know the many shortcuts veteran soldiers knew; shortcuts that made life more bearable in the army. They were simple things, like sleeping with your musket covered to reduce the rust that inevitably formed on the barrel, and peeing just before bed so you wouldn't be so desperate to do so in the morning when it was cold and miserable. After all, there was no room for chamber pots in the army. If one needed to relieve himself, he had to face the harshness of the outdoors to use the latrines that were dug on the edge of camp to prevent sickness. To do otherwise was a violation of orders.

These lessons and a hundred more revealed themselves to John over time. He would learn the skills of army life the way the veterans had—through experience.

The lessons continued when Colonel Buford marched his detachment out of Petersburg on March 29th. There was no ride in a wagon for John on this march. Loaded with barrels of gunpowder, lead ball, provisions, tents and poles, and other supplies and gear, there was no room for *anyone* in the wagons. The men had to march carrying their packs and muskets, reducing the burden on the draft horses who had to haul the heavy wagons, supplies, and camp gear over four hundred miles to Charleston. John updated James on his situation in early April.

April 2, 1780

Dear James,

I received your favor dated March 19th just before we left Petersburg and am pleased to learn that all is well in Yorktown. I write to you after a long day of marching. We left Petersburg four days ago on a march to Charleston that I've been told is over four hundred miles away. My last two weeks in camp were no more eventful than my first two, except that we finally received our coats. Most everyone now wears a blue, thigh length, light wool coat with red facings down the front and on the collar and cuffs. They appear shabbily made, but are warm, perhaps too warm for where we are marching. We all wear cocked hats and there is a mix of breeches and overalls among the men, some four hundred strong including the officers. The officers are dressed fine, but many of the men remain in poor condition. My overalls are in better shape than most, and I still have another pair and my breeches in my pack. In fact, I am one of the better supplied soldiers, fortunate to have two shirts and two pairs of stockings in my pack with my extra trousers and breeches. My shoes are also in good condition, although I expect this long march may change that. Many of the men have worn out shoes, and some prefer to go barefoot.

We only march about ten miles each day, slowed by a train of artillery and baggage. We sleep under the stars, wrapped in our blankets most nights, and only set up our tents when the weather is bad. Six men to a tent is not comfortable, but it is warmer than sleeping under the stars, so I don't mind it. The blankets are thin and small, and I need to use some of mine to wrap around my musket, which leaves little left for me.

A party of camp followers trails behind, wives and children of some of the soldiers. They are in wretched condition and I feel sorry for them, but they say they have no choice, they have nothing to sustain them at home. They do provide a service for the troops, they launder and mend our clothes, for which they receive enough provision to survive. But it is a hard life and I pity them, especially the children.

We are told that General Clinton has a large force outside of Charleston, but there are still avenues open to the city which we may use to reinforce the army. General Lincoln commands there. He was second in command at Saratoga, so one expects that Charleston is in good hands.

We are well supplied with provisions and my French musket is in good order, but my feet hurt, as I am sure you remember.

I have made many acquaintances and admire my comrades. Many are seasoned veterans, and although they sometimes tease me, they also offer advice. I am particularly fond of Sergeant Ballard and Sergeant Baley. Both are fine men and we are lucky to have them in the company. Captain Wallace is also an excellent commander, admired by all in the company.

Have you heard from Father or Rebecca lately? I imagine business is slow at the tavern. I hope all is well with you and General Nelson's family. Write to me soon with an update. Until then, I remain,

Your Loving and Obedient Brother,

John

When they reached Hillsborough, North Carolina, John left his letter with Mr. Jonathan West, whom he discovered was traveling to Richmond. Mr. West kindly agreed to deliver the letter—along with a shorter one John had quickly written to Rebecca—to Anderson's Tavern in Richmond. He refused to accept payment for his trouble and told John he hoped to be in Richmond within a week. The plan was for Rebecca to receive both letters and then forward James's letter to Yorktown.

Colonel Buford was forced to remain in Hillsborough for two more days as he waited for the rain to end and stragglers to catch up. But the march resumed on April 11th and continued daily for two hundred miles until they reached Camden, South Carolina on April 25th. Hoping to find someone in the town who was heading north toward Virginia, John composed another, longer letter to Rebecca.

April 25, 1780

Dear Becca,

I have not heard from you since your last letter on March 23rd, but I do not fault you for I am sure you have written me since. We have marched daily so it would be folly for me to expect that a letter from Richmond could find me so quickly when we re-locate ourselves every day.

We have stopped in Camden, South Carolina, a fine town. Our marches have not been too demanding, less than fifteen miles a day, but after nearly three weeks of it, my feet are as beat up as my shoes, which have worn considerably.

Our spirits are high, and if I weren't so tired and sore, I would find all of this traveling interesting. James was right about the army though; it is far less exciting than I imagined.

I am fortunate to have formed a friendship with a veteran sergeant who looks out for me. Sergeant Ballard is from Hampton and has served for five years. He knows Father, visited the Raleigh frequently before the war, and remembers me from when I was a child. He has taught me a lot of tricks to make life less miserable in the army and I appreciate his kindness.

He thinks we will be here in Camden for several days because the detachment is so stretched out with stragglers. It may take that long for them to catch up. It has also begun to rain hard, which soaks the sandy roads soft and makes it more difficult to move the heavy wagons.

We have learned very little of how Charleston fares. I expect though that its defenses will hold and we shall resist the enemy as we did in '76.

How are your parents and sister? Has the tavern been as busy as your father wished? Have you heard from James or anyone from Williamsburg? I wonder how the city fares.

I expect by the time you receive this letter we will be in Charleston, so I would address your reply to that city.

In the meantime, know that I am safe and that I miss our visits to the brook.

I am, as always, your Affectionate Friend,

John

What John did not know when he wrote to Rebecca, was that a letter from General Lincoln was waiting for Colonel Buford in Camden with orders to proceed to Charleston as quickly as possible. So, Buford's troops rested in Camden for just one night before they were on the move again.

As they marched, John heard whispers about Charleston that concerned him. The British navy had fought their way past the American fort on Sullivan's Island and was in Charleston Harbor, tightening their siege on the city. All the roads in and out of Charleston had been severed by the British, and it was only a matter of time before the five thousand American troops—including nearly all of Virginia's Continentals—were forced to surrender.

When Colonel Buford and his detachment reached Lenud's Ferry on May 6th, just forty miles north of Charleston on the Santee River, the colonel heard directly from several South Carolina officials, including Governor John Rutledge, that Charleston was doomed. With all the roads to Charleston blocked by the British, Buford was uncertain how to proceed.

Brigadier-General Isaac Huger of South Carolina—who was out of the city when the British sealed off Charleston—arrived on May 8th, and informed Colonel Buford that it was useless for the Virginians to march on.

"General Lincoln will surrender any day now, if he hasn't already, and your detachment is far too weak to prevent it. You are to turn back and march to Hillsborough where you will meet new reinforcements coming south from General Washington's army."

Colonel Buford took in the grim news, keeping it to himself for a few hours before forming the detachment late in the day to explain the situation. He stood before the entire detachment, looking from left to right, a serious, determined look on his face.

The silence made John uncomfortable and he thought to himself, *this is going to be bad.* He looked to Sergeant Ballard for reassurance, but the sergeant stood silent and ramrod straight at attention, staring forward. Finally, Colonel Buford addressed the men.

"I am told that General Lincoln and his army are trapped in Charleston and that we are too few to make any difference. General Huger and I refuse to needlessly throw your lives away, therefore, we shall march north and unite with reinforcements from General Washington. Rest assured, however, we will avenge our comrades in Charleston. Company commanders, take command of your men and prepare them to march in the morning!" Colonel Buford then faced about and returned to his quarters.

Captain Wallace stepped forward and faced his company. "I want everyone to have rations for three days cooked by nightfall. We have a lot of marching to do so get as much rest as you can tonight. Company, dismissed!"

It was a somber group of men with John who cooked their salt pork and cornmeal late in the afternoon. Each seemed consumed with their own thoughts when George

Nipper, a veteran of the old 6th Virginia Regiment, broke the silence.

"Colonel Buford is a good man. If he says it is hopeless to march to Charleston, I'm sure it is."

"I don't know," replied William Champ, a new recruit like John, but several years older. "Feels kind of cowardly to me to march away from Charleston after we've come so far."

"Clinton has eight thousand men! What can we do against that?" Nipper countered.

"I agree with Champ, it seems pointless to have marched all this way only to turn around and march back," said Isham Burks, a draftee from the militia.

John, who was uncharacteristically silent during most of the discussion, smiled at the last point. *Just like James in Smithfield,* he thought. He stayed out of the conversation and turned in as soon as the last of his salt pork and cornmeal had been cooked into hard little cakes.

The detachment commenced its march north before sunrise the next day. Three days later, on May 12th, General Lincoln in Charleston surrendered his army and the city to the British. It marked the worst American defeat of the war.

General Clinton, flush with victory, learned of Buford's withdrawal shortly after the American surrender and ordered General Charles Cornwallis to pursue them. Cornwallis led troops inland and sent a detachment of two hundred and seventy mounted soldiers under the command of Lieutenant Colonel Banastre Tarleton to ride ahead to slow the Virginians. They ended up doing far more than that, however.

When Colonel Buford reached Camden on May 26th, he loaded his twenty-six wagons—whose loads had diminished along the long march south—as full as possible with gunpowder and other military supplies that had been stored in Camden. His goal was to prevent the British from seizing the supplies themselves. Slowed by the weight of the re-loaded wagons, he continued north.

Colonel Tarleton, unencumbered by baggage wagons, pushed his men and horses hard, covering the last one hundred and five miles in only fifty-four hours. He caught up with Colonel Buford near a settlement called Waxhaws on May 29th. Situated near the border of North and South Carolina, the coming fight would prove disastrous for the Virginians.

John and his comrades were completely unaware that the enemy were pursuing them, but Colonel Buford had been warned the day before. He was not concerned however, figuring it must be a small party of cavalry that his men could easily fend off. He did nothing to increase the pace of his march, so by the early afternoon a lone British officer on horseback had caught up to them with a demand to surrender. Tarleton had sent him forward in hopes of delaying Buford, but the American commander rejected the demand without stopping.

Word that the British were near swept along the American column. John tensed at the news. *This is it,* he thought, *my first battle*.

The Virginians kept marching and traveled two miles further before gunfire was heard in their rear. A small party of mounted Virginians—the rear guard of Buford's column—was attacked and overwhelmed by Tarleton's force. They were just a half mile behind and closing fast.

Colonel Buford ordered his column to halt and deploy for battle. A small guard continued forward with the baggage wagons and cannons, and John wished for a moment that he was with them, but Captain Wallace snapped him back to the issue at hand, repeating Colonel Buford's order to deploy into a battle line.

Three hundred and fifty Virginians moved quickly to form two long lines facing the enemy. John stood in the rear rank behind an older, but shorter, soldier named Caleb. Normally, the men in both ranks would have stood shoulder to shoulder as a compact wall of soldiers two lines deep. But Colonel Buford was concerned that the enemy would sweep around the ends of his line and flank them, so he ordered the men to deploy in open order, with a two-foot gap between each man. This extended the battleline considerably but would prove to be the first of two crucial mistakes Buford would make.

Although deploying in open order *had* made his line much longer, it also made it weaker and easier to break with a direct assault. Had Buford formed his men at close order—shoulder to shoulder—they would have formed a stronger wall of soldiers, many with bayonets on the end of their muskets, and that would have been harder for Tarleton's cavalry to attack. In the rush to deploy, however, Buford chose the wrong formation, and his detachment paid dearly for it.

Colonel Tarleton was not the sort of officer to bother with flanking movements anyway—he was a hard charging leader, and he stayed true to form at Waxhaws. He ordered his exhausted force to charge straight at the Virginians, who outnumbered him by nearly a hundred men.

John was posted near the left flank of the American line and watched with unease and—he hated to admit—admiration, as Tarleton's horsemen charged straight at them. He had read about such charges before in history, but none of the accounts captured what he saw and felt. The sound of over two hundred horses riding in formation straight at him unnerved John. The rumble of their hooves grew louder and louder.

Why aren't we firing? he wondered, a sense of panic replacing the awe as the charging horsemen drew closer. *Give the order…give the bloody order*, urged John to himself, desperately wanting to fire and stop their charge.

But the officers and sergeants, following Colonel Buford's command, repeatedly shouted, "Hold, hold, hold your fire. Stand firm and hold your fire!"

This is insane, thought John. *Why don't we fire*?

Colonel Buford rode along the back of the battleline encouraging the men. John heard him cry out, "Easy boys, let them get closer." A few of the men couldn't resist and disobeyed, firing early, but most—including John—reluctantly complied and waited for the order to fire.

This would be Colonel Buford's second mistake. He had waited too long to fire upon the enemy. They were a mere ten yards away when he finally gave the command to fire. The result was a catastrophe for the Virginians.

John squeezed the trigger, closing his eyes in response to the flash of gunpowder that ignited in the pan of the musket. The roar of muskets was deafening and he and his comrades were enveloped in smoke.

The volley they fired smashed into the lead dragoons of Tarleton's cavalry, dropping horse and men alike, but those who followed were unscathed and crashed into the Virginia line, sabers swinging wildly upon their heads.

My God, thought John when Caleb suddenly spun around and collapsed to the ground, his head nearly severed by an enemy saber. John crouched down instinctively and used his musket to deflect a saber meant for him, but the blade caught his left hand, cutting him badly. The rider reared his horse to the left and struck another soldier further down the line.

The Virginia line had been smashed, but mixed among shouts for mercy and cries for help, John heard Sergeant Ballard's booming voice urging the men to hold the line. *What line, where did everyone go?* John thought as he stood up and looked around wildly, musket at the ready despite the gash on his left hand. He was terrified that a British saber would strike him at any moment. *I can't stay here*, he thought as he turned to run away. But as he did, Sergeant Ballard appeared in front of him.

"Easy, lad, easy, hold your ground," Sergeant Ballard calmly commanded before redirecting John to the front. "Use your bayonet, son."

"Sergeant Ballard!" shouted Captain Wallace, bloodied by the enemy charge. "Get this line reformed in close order!"

Calls to reform were shouted and John realized that most of the company had indeed held. They had bent, but had not broken. The same could not be said for Buford's center or right sections of the line, however. The center had borne the brunt of the attack and was smashed and scattered. The right flank had also been shattered, but enough men remained to offer some resistance.

John realized that he hadn't reloaded, so he reached for a cartridge, but it was too late. The enemy dragoons were upon them again. Two came at John simultaneously from each side. He deflected the saber of the dragoon on his right with his musket, but the dragoon on his left caught him on the left forearm, and as John recoiled from that he was struck again on the head behind his left ear.

John dropped to his knees, unable to use his musket. Sergeant Ballard, who was himself bleeding from a saber wound to the head, ordered John to go to the rear—but John wasn't sure the rear was any safer than the front. There were enemy horsemen all around, and they were incensed because their commander, Colonel Tarleton, had fallen in battle—or so they believed.

Realizing the battle was lost and that the enemy were taking no prisoners, Sergeant Ballard grabbed John's right arm and lifted him to his feet.

"Run, lad, run for your life!" he urged with a look of concern for John. He cast John rearward and then turned to fight on.

Fear swept over John, but he did as he was told. There was a cluster of trees about thirty yards away to the left that he ran toward, holding his bloody left arm with his right hand. When he got there, he stopped and looked back.

The enemy hadn't noticed him—they were focused on the remnants of Buford's line. John watched in horror as fellow Virginians, many with arms raised in surrender, were cut down by British sabers.

John's stomach dropped. *They're not taking prisoner*s, he thought, horrified at the realization. *They're killing everyone.*

He turned and ran toward more woods fifty yards away. His left arm and hand ached and he bled profusely, but he kept running, terrified that at any moment he'd be cut down by a British saber.

Behind him lay over three hundred Virginians, killed and grievously wounded at the hands of troops led by Colonel Banastre Tarleton. The British commander had been unhorsed in the battle but he emerged unscathed and victorious. The ruthless conduct of some of his men towards the Virginians, however, earned him a new nickname, "Bloody Tarleton."

Chapter Eleven

The Army Reforms in Hillsborough

June 1780

After what seemed like an eternity of running, John emerged in a clearing and saw a small house with corn planted around it in the distance. Still holding his left arm with his right hand, he walked to the house and banged on the door with his uninjured arm.

"Dear Lord," exclaimed the woman who opened the door. "Come in quickly. Here, sit, let me tend to your wounds."

She grabbed a basin and filled it from the well outside, then returned, took what looked like an old linen shirt, and ripped it into strips. She soaked one of the strips and began wiping John's cuts. Some of the blood had already dried and stuck to his skin so when she tore it away the cuts began to bleed again. Quickly, she took two wider strips of linen and bound them around the cuts to stop the bleeding.

"Are you hurt anywhere else?" she asked.

“My head is throbbing in the back,” John replied. “I think I was cut there too.”

The woman tipped John’s head forward gingerly to check. “You certainly were—there is a gash above your ear.” She cleaned the cut, put a clean strip of linen on it, and told John to hold it in place with his good hand.

She then went back to the well to fill another bucket of water. She poured some in a tin cup when she returned. “Here, have a drink, son.”

John nodded in appreciation and gulped the water down. It tasted good. She refilled the cup and he drank that just as fast.

Just then the door opened and the woman’s husband entered. He had seen John come to the door from the cornfield. “Were you in the battle?” he asked, fully aware that he was. “We heard the shooting for a bit. Who won?”

John hesitated. He worried that his benefactors might be Tories who would report him to the British or worse—dispatch him themselves.

“I’m not sure,” he replied, unable to meet the man’s eyes. “I fled because of these wounds.”

"Well, you look to be a Continental, so we better hide you in case the British come looking for you. No telling what they will do if they catch you."

John let out a sigh of relief. It appeared the couple was friendly to the patriot cause. "I was with Colonel Buford's detachment from Virginia," he confessed. "We were marching north when British dragoons caught us."

"You poor thing," crooned the woman. "You look too young to be a soldier. How old are you, son?"

"Sixteen, ma'am."

"And your name?" asked her husband.

"John Southall, I'm from Williamsburg, sir."

"Our name is Cain. George and Sarah Cain," the man said, motioning toward his wife, who smiled at John. Mr. Cain glanced at John's arm and his brows knitted together with concern. "We'll look after you for a bit as you're in no condition to fend for yourself. Come, let's get you up in the loft so you can rest."

He helped John up the ladder to the loft. Mrs. Cain passed a chunk of bread and ham up with another cup of water.

"You just rest a bit," said Mr. Cain as he descended the latter. "I'll go out and see if any redcoats are snooping around."

When John went to lay down, he realized he was still wearing his pack. The veterans in his company had warned him never to remove it in battle, else he would likely lose it. *They were right*, he thought. *If I had laid it aside to fight like many others had, it would still be there on the ground.* He took the pack off to use it as a pillow and was asleep within minutes of resting his head.

John awoke with a start and for a moment, forgot where he was. There was a slight sweet smell in the air, and a sizzling sound. He realized someone was cooking and then remembered—the Cains. He leaned toward the opening of the loft and looked down.

"Ah, there you are," said Mr. Cain. "You slept right through dinner, but we thought we'd cook you some supper before we turned in."

"Thank you kindly," replied John. "It smells delicious." He carefully climbed down the ladder and took a seat at the table. The house was only a one room building with a loft, so he was a mere few feet from the fireplace and could see what looked like a stew cooking over the flames.

Mrs. Cain was stirring the stew. “Let me look at your wounds,” she said, stepping away from the pot. She looked at his head first, then his hand and arm. The bleeding had stopped for all three, and a thick layer of dried blood now covered each gash. She gave John’s arm a gentle pat. “Let’s leave the wounds alone for tonight. We’ll re-dress them tomorrow.”

Mrs. Cain rose and fetched a bowl and spoon for John. “Should be about ready now,” she said as she removed the pot from the fire. The stew smelled heavenly and John made quick work of it, thanking the couple profusely in between bites.

“What are your plans, son?” Mr. Cain asked.

John thought for a moment. “Well, we were marching back to Hillsborough, so I suppose I should continue on to there.”

Mr. Cain’s eyes widened. “That’s a mighty long walk from here, lad. At least a hundred and fifty miles.”

John grimaced, remembering the journey. “Oh, I know, sir. We walked it just a few weeks ago, but that is where I expect to find my unit and I ought to return to them."

Mr. Cain said nothing, just nodded.

"When will you start out?" Mrs. Cain asked.

"Well, if I can stay here tonight," John started sheepishly, "I'd like to start in the morning."

"Why of course you can stay tonight," Mrs. Cain tutted. "You can stay as long as you need to."

"I'm much obliged, but I think one night will do." He motioned at his bandaged arm. "You've patched me up quite nicely, I don't expect I will need more than another night's rest."

Mrs. Cain smiled. "Say nothing of it."

"You can sleep right here, next to the fire," said Mr. Cain.

John bowed his head. "Thank you both."

The fire was warm, but John slept restlessly, his wounds—despite Mrs. Cain's tender care—throbbed and ached. He awoke at dawn to the sound of Mrs. Cain stirring the embers.

"Good morning, son. Did you get much sleep?"

"Yes, ma'am," he said as he rubbed the sleep from his eyes. In truth, he hadn't slept well at all, but he did not want to complain. Mrs. Cain noticed his discomfort, however. It was obvious in the slow, careful way he moved his injured arm, and the twitch in his eye when the pain flared.

"Let's have a look at those cuts and clean them up," Mrs. Cain said, her eyes on his arm. She already had a basin of clean water and strips of linen waiting on the table. When she unwrapped John's bandages, the cloth stuck to the dried blood and pulled. He inhaled sharply at the pain, his eyes stinging. "I'm sorry, son, but they need to come off," Mrs. Cain said gently.

Afraid his voice would betray him, John only nodded.

After all the cloth had been removed, Mrs. Cain cleaned each wound with water. "They look good, no putrid smell or puss," she said cheerily, then wrapped his hand and arm in new strips of cloth. She thought of trying to wrap some linen around John's head and chin to cover his wound, but his hair and dried blood had matted enough to create an adequate cover to stop the bleeding, so she let it be.

"Let's get you some breakfast," she said when she finished.

As John waited at the table, Mr. Cain descended from the loft and asked how John fared.

"Well, sir, all things considered," John replied. "Mrs. Cain has fixed me up nicely, and I am indebted to both of you for your kindness."

"Nonsense," replied Mr. Cain. "It is we who are indebted to you. To be so young and in the army. God bless you, son. God bless you."

John smiled at the sentiment and watched as Mrs. Cain cooked up some hoecakes over the fire. When they were ready, he gobbled them down so quickly he feared he'd burned his tongue. The Cains offered him some water to help, which he accepted gratefully, thanking the couple again for their hospitality.

"I must be off," he said as he stood from the table and retrieved his pack.

The Cains nodded. "You'll be passing through Salisbury on your way," said Mr. Cain, "and may catch a ride from there. Wagons pass between there and Hillsborough most every day."

"How far away is Salisbury?" asked John.

"About sixty miles."

John's feet ached at the news, but he made for the door.

Mrs. Cain approached, her arms full. "There," she said, "this should get you at least halfway to Salisbury."

She had cooked up a large batch of hoecakes, added some corn bread and a half loaf of wheat bread, wrapped some salt pork and filled a small cloth bag with dried fruit, and another bag with a few pickled vegetables.

"Be sure to eat these first," she said as she handed John the pickled vegetables. "Else you'll find them unappealing in a day or two." She then took John's canteen and filled it with water.

John thanked the Cains again for their generosity and kindness and started his journey to Salisbury. He tried to avoid people as much as possible, worried that they might hold Tory sentiments. He slept under the stars for three nights until he reached Salisbury on the afternoon of June 2nd. His food had run out the day before, so he was famished when he arrived and greatly relieved when he found others from Buford's detachment there.

John didn't know any of the twenty odd soldiers at Salisbury. All were survivors of the fight at Waxhaws, but none were from his company. He thought of Sergeant Ballard, who had ordered him to run, and of Sergeant Baley, a veteran of so many previous battles. *What happened to them?* he wondered.

Suddenly, a voice came from behind him. "Who are you?" John turned to see a lieutenant, his brow furrowed with concern.

"John Southall, sir."

"And whose company are you in?"

"Captain Wallace's."

The lieutenant frowned. "Well, you're with me now. I'm Lieutenant Pearson."

"What happened to Captain Wallace?"

The lieutenant hesitated. "He fell at Waxhaws with most of his company. Looks like you almost fell, too." He gestured to John's head. "You better have a doctor look at your wounds."

John asked one of the soldiers where he could find a doctor, and was directed to a tavern adjacent to the courthouse. As he approached, he heard screams from inside and paused at the steps. The screaming subsided and a window on the side of the tavern burst open. John was horrified to see the person inside toss an arm out the window. It landed on a small pile of limbs—legs and feet, arms and hands—that had been thrown out previously.

"Good God!" John said under his breath as he stood frozen in front of the tavern, clutching his wounded arm tighter.

Suddenly, the front door opened and a sergeant emerged. He saw John standing still, gripping his wounded arm tightly.

"Get in here and see the doctor, lad," said the sergeant. "Come on, let's go."

But John didn't move. The sergeant traced John's gaze to the pile of limbs and then looked back at John and shook his head. *Shock,* he thought. He walked up and shook John gently. "Come on, son. You need to see the doctor. It will be all right."

John snapped out of his trance and followed the sergeant, dreading what might come next.

"Got another one doctor," announced the sergeant as they entered the tavern.

"Have him wait, I'll be with him soon," the doctor called from a nearby room.

After a few minutes the doctor approached. He wore a blood-soaked apron and held a rag which he wiped his hands with in a futile attempt to clean them.

"Let's look at those wounds, son." He unwrapped the dressing and looked closely at John's hand and arm. It was too late to stitch up either cut, but both seemed to be healing fine without stitches.

"Your hand looks good, but there is a little putridness in your arm. We'll clean it and leave it uncovered for a bit before we re-dress it. Are you hurt anywhere else?"

"My head, sir, I have a cut on my head."

The doctor pointed at a nearby stool. "Sit over here, let me look at it."

He ran his fingers through John's hair and picked at the dried blood that covered the wound. John grimaced as the doctor picked and picked, and just when John thought he couldn't take it anymore, the doctor stopped and patted his shoulder. "You are a fortunate soldier, lad," he said. "Your wounds are healing nicely. We'll want to keep an eye on that arm though. I'll wrap it with clean cloth in an hour."

Lieutenant Pearson had returned to check on John and overheard the doctor. "So, he'll be able to march with us tomorrow?"

"His arm will be in a sling, so he can't carry a musket," the doctor started, "but yes, he's well enough to travel."

Lieutenant Pearson patted John on the shoulder. "Fine, fine, then you're off with us to Hillsborough tomorrow."

They left early the next morning with three wagons and twenty-three men, most wounded in some way. It was a repeat of his first march with the army—from Williamsburg to Petersburg. There was not enough room in the wagons for everyone to ride, so as usual those who could walk took turns walking alongside. They camped in the open under the stars and arrived in Hillsborough after four days. Midway through the journey, John grew feverish, and Lieutenant Pearson worried that his arm had become infected. There was no doctor with them, however, so as John grew worse, all Lieutenant Pearson could do was allow John to ride in a wagon the rest of the way.

When they reached Hillsborough on June 6th, John was taken to a makeshift hospital and examined by another doctor.

"Smallpox!" the doctor announced after a brief examination. "He needs to be quarantined immediately. What of the men he was with?" he asked Lieutenant Pearson. "They'll need to be examined, and if any have never had it or not been inoculated for it, they'll need to be quarantined as well."

John heard the discussion but was dizzy with fever. He tried to clear his throat to speak, but before he could the doctor had turned from him. "Abigail," the doctor called, "come take this lad to the Henderson's. And be sure to keep him away from everyone on the way."

Abigail Jenkins was the doctor's 16-year-old daughter. She had been inoculated for smallpox several years earlier so her father was not worried that she would contract it from John.

Suddenly, there was a pressure on his right arm. John rolled his head toward it and made out a small, delicate hand—*a girl's,* he thought, but the strength behind it confused him. The hand pulled him closer and he leaned against the side of her body, allowing her to steady him. "You're all right," a warm voice sounded in his ears. John tilted his head up and peeked golden hair. He tried to catch a better look, but the world around him wouldn't stop spinning.

"Where are we going?" he mumbled as she led him down the main street of Hillsborough.

"The Henderson's place. They're Tories, long since gone. We use their house for quarantine cases like yours. There's been no call to use it since February though."

The house was just a short walk away, but John was fading fast as they climbed the steps to the door. He tried once more to get a better look at his rescuer and thought he glanced green eyes, but couldn't be sure.

"Aren't you afraid of catching it?" he asked weakly as she brought him to a room with a bed.

She shook her head and a golden wave tumbled loose from behind her ear. "I was inoculated years ago," she tucked the renegade strand back. "So, I can't catch it again."

John wanted to talk more with her, but as she helped him into the bed everything grew heavier. He fought to keep his eyes open, but it was a losing battle. He collapsed onto the bed and drifted into sleep.

Chapter Twelve

What News of John?

Summer 1780

Rebecca and her family found life in Richmond extremely hectic. Although the tavern Mr. Anderson had rented from Abraham Crowley was not as large or grand as the Wetherburn Tavern in Williamsburg, it was large enough to keep the family and their servants very busy. This was especially true because of a severe shortage of housing in the new capital. Mr. Anderson's tavern, like the other taverns in Richmond, turned away guests almost every night from April until June while the state Assembly was in session.

As Rebecca's father had expected, their move to Richmond proved very profitable—made doubly so by Mr. Anderson's excellent reputation as a tavernkeeper in Williamsburg. Many of his former patrons preferred Anderson's Richmond tavern over the other local taverns, and his establishment was frequently overflowing with guests.

Rebecca—who had turned sixteen in late May—divided her time between tutoring her sister and helping her parents with the tavern. She tried to write to James often, especially when they first arrived and she had the time. By May, however, she was overwhelmed with work and had little time for letters. Nevertheless, she managed to write to James at the end of the month.

May 30, 1780

Dearest James,

I have finally managed to steal a moment to write. You cannot imagine how busy things have been since the Assembly opened last month. A multitude of people have descended upon this small town, and people are so desperate for accommodations that gentlemen of rank sometimes sleep upon ticks on the floor alongside their servants.

Richmondtown as it stands now is no Williamsburg, you can be assured of that. There are but a handful of large homes scattered amongst many small wooden tenements. But now that the government has moved here, the town is overwhelmed with visitors, and I expect that someday this place will equal or maybe even surpass Williamsburg.

Father was fortunate to acquire a rather respectable tavern on the Williamsburg Road near the river. It is smaller than our tavern in Williamsburg, but sits next to the courthouse and near where father expects the new government buildings to be built.

For now, the legislators meet in the confiscated home of a Tory who has long since abandoned his property. I know not how they squeeze everyone into the building, for it is but a fraction of the size of the old Capitol.

I have not received a letter from John in several weeks and worry, for the news from Charleston is grim. I received your letters of May 3rd and 9th and am pleased your lessons continue to go well.

Father says that I may be able to visit Williamsburg in the summer once the Assembly adjourns. Uncle James is moving his armory to Richmond and comes back and forth from home frequently. My hope is that in July I can return to Williamsburg and stay with him. I will write again when our plans are set. I do hope though that you might manage to visit while I am there. Visiting our brook alone would be difficult.

Please convey my warmest regards to your family, and know that you remain my dearest friend.

Your Loving and Affectionate,

Becca

Rebecca's next letter to James two weeks later carried a much different tone. It was frantic and brief. Reports of the disaster at Waxhaws reached Richmond in mid-June and put Rebecca into a panic.

June 14, 1780

Dearest James,

I know not what to do. The town is full of stories of the defeat of Colonel Buford's men in South Carolina. John was with them! They apparently did not reach Charleston before General Lincoln surrendered the town and had started to march back here when they were caught by British dragoons.

The accounts are awful. It seems the dragoons cut down everyone, even those who tried to surrender. Poor John, I don't know what I will do if we've lost him. Please, please write to me if you learn anything. Perhaps General Nelson can help.

The Assembly had adjourned before the news arrived—else I would have questioned every gentleman I met. Alas, all I can do is pray and hope that John survived the horrible massacre. I remain,

Your Loving Rebecca.

James had learned about the battle at Waxhaws from General Nelson the day before Rebecca's letter arrived. The details were sketchy, yet alarming. Buford's command had been wiped out, that much was clear. Many were killed and wounded, though it seemed some had been captured unhurt, but those numbers were uncertain. Buford himself and about fifty men reportedly escaped—but who these lucky men were remained unknown.

James did not share these details with Rebecca. He replied in a letter that there was no report about John specifically, so there was no reason to believe he was hurt— or worse. *The odds aren't on his side,* thought James as he wrote, *but there's no need to cause Becca more worry.*

More than a month passed before they finally learned that John had been wounded but had survived the battle and escaped capture. By then, James and Rebecca were in Williamsburg for a week-long visit together. Rebecca was staying with her aunt, who had remained in Williamsburg after her husband had moved the armory to Richmond.

Rebecca received the news about John first. He had written to her from Hillsborough and her father had forwarded his letter to Williamsburg.

"He's alive, James! Wounded and sick, but alive!" she joyously reported as she waved John's letter about. "He's been in Hillsborough all this time."

The letter Rebecca held had been written two weeks earlier—only after John had passed the dangerous part of his illness. The worst of this ordeal had lasted a week. John had suffered days of high fever and delirium; his body covered with pustules full of the smallpox virus.

When his fever had finally subsided and he'd regained his senses, he awoke to someone wiping his forehead with a cool wet cloth. He slowly opened his eyes.

"There you are," said the blurred vision above him when she noticed he'd awakened.

John blinked and squinted to see, but didn't recognize the person before him. "What happened?" he whispered.

"You've been terribly ill," came the reply.

John looked side to side, still confused, his vision still blurry. He heard water being poured in a cup and struggled to sit up, desperate to have a drink. He felt hands reach around him and lift him toward the end of the bed, sitting him up. He squinted intently and could see that it was a girl with blonde hair. She handed John the cup and he gulped the water down quickly. There was a low chuckle and then she took the cup from him and went to re-fill it.

"How long have I been sick?" he asked.

"Nearly two weeks. But the worst is over now, your fever's broke."

John looked down at his hands, then moved his sleeves up to see his arms. A smattering of red scabs ran up both arms. "Smallpox?"

The girl nodded. "Yes, a bad case of it." She motioned toward the scabs. "But those will fade in time, don't worry."

John reddened, embarrassed that she thought he cared about the scars. "Did you take care of me all this time?" he asked.

The girl smiled. "With the help of my father and Sally."

John forced himself to look at her, embarrassment be damned. "I am indebted to—" he stopped, startled by her beauty. Then he remembered—a gleam of gold, a flash of green. "I-I remember you… you're the doctor's daughter."

"Abigail Jenkins," she said with a smile and a curtsey.

"You helped me here," John recalled, the memory still fuzzy, but he was sure now it had been her. "Has it really been two weeks?"

Abigail shrugged. "Like I said, you were pretty sick."

Just then, Doctor Jenkins entered the room and Abigail rose to greet her father.

"So, our young patient is finally awake. You had us worried, lad."

John tried to sit up straighter and winced. *I hope she didn't notice that,* he thought as his eyes darted to Abigail. But her eyes stayed fixed on her father. John cleared his throat. "I believe I have you and your daughter to thank for my care," he said.

"Yes, my Abigail is quite gifted," replied the doctor with a smile at his daughter. Abigail blushed and fixed her gaze at her feet.

Doctor Jenkins moved toward John. "Come now, let me see your head." John sat up and leaned forward to allow him to inspect his wound. "Very good, very good," he said. "And now your arm and hand."

John held out his left arm for inspection.

"Your wounds have healed nicely, son. And you've passed through the worst of the pox, so you should be up and about in a few days. Until then though, you must remain quarantined." He turned to his daughter and said with a smile, "you will continue to tend to him I assume, as you've yet to leave his side."

Abigail's eyes widened and her cheeks flamed. "Just doing my duty, Father," she said with a curtsey.

"I must be off then. Be sure to get him to drink some broth, and as much water as possible. Tomorrow he can try some solid food."

Abigail left with her father but returned with a bowl of broth. "Doctor's orders," she said as she handed the bowl to John. "Be sure to drink it all."

"That won't be a problem," John said as he lifted the bowl to his lips, "I'm famished."

After his second bowl, John asked for more water and his pack.

Abigail returned with both. "You're recovering quite nicely," she said as she handed John the cup. "And you've been a model patient."

John smiled; he had rarely been called a model anything before.

"Do you live here in Hillsborough?" he asked.

"I do. Born and raised here, just my father and I."

What about your mother? John wondered, to which Abigail volunteered an answer, as if she had read his mind.

"My mother died when I was young, so it's been just my father and I ever since."

"I'm sorry," John said softly.

"It's all right," she said. "I don't have many memories of her, so it's hard to really miss her." She tilted her head to the side and tucked a stray strand of hair behind her ear. "And what about your family? Where do they live?"

"They are in Williamsburg. My father owns a tavern there."

"Do they know that you are well?"

John swallowed, thinking of how worried his family must be. "Probably not."

"Well, we must correct that. Here, let me help you up to the table. It's time to write to them."

Abigail took John's hands as he swung his feet to the floor. He was about to rise with her help when he realized that he only had a nightshirt on.

"Wait!" he cried. "I-I'm not properly dressed."

Abigail laughed. "Oh please, how do you think you got that clean shirt on?"

John was stunned at the thought, but felt Abigail struggling to lift him to his feet, so he rose, red in the face with embarrassment. Abigail put her arm around his waist and he draped his good arm over her shoulder, and together they made their way to the table.

But John felt queasy and faint, and had started to grow heavy on her, so Abigail quickly realized he was not well enough to sit and write. "Change of plans," she said as she guided John around and back to his bed. "We'll try to write another time."

John was relieved at her decision and settled back into his bed. "Yes, another time," he said, closing his eyes to halt the spinning.

"You get more rest now. I'll check on you later," Abigail instructed. Then she picked up the empty bowl and left the room.

Several days later, released from quarantine but still ordered to rest, Colonel Charles Porterfield paid John a visit. Colonel Porterfield was a large man of thirty, and a veteran of the war. He had marched to Boston as an ensign with Daniel Morgan, the famous Virginia rifle commander in 1775. Captain Morgan's rifle company had joined Colonel Benedict Arnold on his march to Canada in the fall of that year and Porterfield had stormed the barricades of Quebec in a blizzard with Morgan in a failed attempt to capture the city. Arnold had been wounded in the leg at the start of the attack and forced to withdraw, but Morgan, accompanied by Porterfield and the rest of Arnold's force, had fought hard and nearly breached Quebec's defenses. Alas, the enemy held, and most of Arnold's men—including Captain Morgan and Ensign Porterfield—had been captured.

Imprisoned for seven months in the city, Porterfield fell ill with smallpox and nearly died. But by the summer, he had been paroled by the British and returned to Virginia, where he learned that he had been exchanged and could serve in the army once more. Having then been promoted to captain, he commanded his own company of riflemen under newly promoted Colonel Morgan. Porterfield had fought at Brandywine and Germantown, had served at Valley Forge, and had been promoted to major and then lieutenant-colonel of a Virginia State Garrison regiment in 1778.

When the British moved against Charleston in early 1780, Governor Jefferson selected Colonel Porterfield to lead reinforcements drawn from his own small regiment and the State Artillery Garrison Regiment. His force numbered four hundred men, and it was this force that was in Hillsborough while John recovered from his illness.

Colonel Porterfield knew John—particularly his father—from his time posted in Williamsburg in 1779 with the State Garrison Regiment.

"You look fine, son. I can barely see any marks of the distemper," Colonel Porterfield said when he entered the room—despite John's very obvious struggle to sit up in the bed. Colonel Porterfield helped him slide back against the wall and then took a seat next to the bed.

"I caught smallpox in Quebec and nearly died from it. Miss Jenkins said you had a rough time of it as well, but the worst is over."

"I don't remember much of it," John replied, "except the cursed scabs."

"Well, they've dried up nicely. Can barely tell you were ill," assured Colonel Porterfield. "You know, I know your father pretty well, and I remember you at the Raleigh."

"And I remember you, sir."

"How are your parents?"

"They are fine," John replied. "Or, at least they were when I left in March."

"You should write home as soon as you can," said Colonel Porterfield. "Your family has likely heard of what happened to Colonel Buford and will fear the worst for you."

"I intend to write to a friend, sir, and will ask her to convey my situation to my family. Miss Rebecca Anderson in Richmond. Her father rented a tavern in Williamsburg until recently."

"Ah, Captain Anderson, of course," replied Colonel Porterfield. "Is she special to you?"

"Yes, sir," said John with a nod. "She is my dearest friend. And she will make sure my parents know that I'm all right."

"Well then, write your letter and I shall send it to Richmond with my next dispatch to the Governor."

"I would be most grateful, sir," said John. "If I may, sir, is Colonel Buford here?"

"He and about fifty men departed over a week ago for Virginia."

"Fifty!" exclaimed John, "that's all that are left?"

Colonel Porterfield nodded gravely. "The enemy refused quarter, at least initially, so many were butchered."

"Do you know if Captain Wallace escaped?"

The colonel let out a soft sigh. "I'm afraid not. I've heard several accounts that he was cut down with most of his company."

John sat silently, staring off into space, consumed with guilt that he had fled and survived—when many in his company had not.

Colonel Porterfield felt the shift in John's demeanor and decided to change the subject. *No good wallowing in the past,* he thought. "Doctor Jenkins says you'll be fit to return to service soon. I suggest that rather than return to Virginia, you remain here with us. Colonel Buford will likely return with more men, and when he does you can re-join his command. But for now, there's no sense to march back and forth, so I propose that you serve under me. Many of my men are leaving soon because their enlistments are up, and I could use you."

John thought for a moment. He wanted revenge for what happened at Waxhaws, but more importantly, he wanted to justify his escape when so many of his comrades had been killed, grievously wounded, or captured. He needed to prove his worth.

Abigail had entered the room as Colonel Porterfield made his request, and the fact that she'd heard it would also factor into John's answer. *She's seen nothing but my weakness,* he thought. *I need to change that.*

"Of course, sir," John said. "I would be honored to serve under your command."

"Very well," said Colonel Porterfield, rising to his feet. "You rest and when you are able, report to Captain Drew's company. He could use you the most."

"Thank you, sir. I shall."

Colonel Porterfield gave one last nod and left.

Abigail cleared her throat from the corner of the room. "Do you feel up to that letter now, Mr. Southall?" she asked.

"I do," he replied. "And I believe I can get to the table on my own." He rose, pausing briefly to get his balance—two weeks in bed had weakened him considerably. Abigail stepped toward him, ready to catch him if he fell, but to John's great relief, he managed to shuffle to the chair and sit.

"Let me get you some ink and paper," Abigail said. "Hold on to the table if you feel dizzy." She left and returned quickly with the items. "Here you go. I will leave you to it. Just call if you need me."

John smiled at her. "Thank you, Abigail."

She returned the smile, noting his informality, which she believed to be a gesture of gratitude. "My pleasure," she said before departing.

John sat and thought for a minute, then began writing.

June 24, 1780

Dear Becca,

I am sure you have heard by now about our defeat in South Carolina. I survived with just a few cuts, and am recovering from smallpox here in Hillsborough. You were right, Becca, I should have been inoculated like you were. It was a difficult illness, but the doctor here says I should fully recover. I owe a great debt to his daughter, who nursed me through the illness. Her name is Abigail and she is quite knowledgeable of medicine. She has spent the past two weeks tending to me.

Colonel Buford has apparently returned to Virginia with just fifty men, all that is left of the nearly four hundred we had when we marched south. I am told Captain Wallace was killed and I fear Sergeant Ballard and Baley, both of whom I mentioned in my last letter, have fallen too. I saw no one from my company before Colonel Buford left, so do not know if anyone other than myself survived.

The army here is reforming under General Baron de Kalb who is expected to arrive any day with troops from Maryland and Delaware sent by General Washington. When Colonel Porterfield's men of the Garrison Regiment are included, we'll have nearly fifteen hundred men. Colonel Porterfield asked me to serve in his detachment and I agreed. We will likely march south in a few days, and hopefully avenge Captain Wallace and those who fell with him.

I tell you Becca, war is not what I thought it to be. It was a horrible sight to see men cut down, and there were several moments that I was sure I was done for. As it is, I have scars on my hand, arm, and head, but they are healing nicely. I'm no longer eager for war and was foolish to ever be so. It's a nasty business and I hope it ends soon. But until it does, I must continue with the army.

Please write to James and my parents and share what I have written, I am sure they are very worried and I regret being the cause of it. I hope you find Richmond tolerable. I miss our time at the brook and pray that one day soon we can all reunite there. Until then, I remain

Your Ever Affectionate Friend,

John

Three days later, John announced to Abigail that he was fully recovered and ready to leave.

Abigail, however, was skeptical. “Are you sure?” she asked. “You’re awfully thin, and you still seem unsteady on your feet.”

“I’m sure,” John insisted. “I can’t possibly thank you enough for your care, Miss Jenkins. You truly saved my life.”

“It’s what I do,” she smiled. “So, you’re welcome.”

John chuckled. “You really are very talented, and I truly am grateful for your care.”

“Pleased to be of service,” she replied with a curtsey.

John was going to bow to her, but he reached out his hand and took hers instead. “Thank you, Abigail.”

Abigail’s hand stiffened in his, but she did not pull away immediately. She rested her piercing green eyes on him for a heartbeat before wiggling from his grasp and turning away. "Just don't go off and get yourself shot or cut up after all my hard work," she huffed, turning back to him. "You're a lot of work John Southall." Her voice was hard, but that undercurrent of warmth was still there, and John swore he saw laughter in her eyes.

He smiled at her, then grabbed his pack and walked out.

Colonel Porterfield was quartered close to the Henderson House and John went straight to him.

"Ready for duty, sir," he said when he was admitted into Porterfield's quarters. He presented the colonel with his letter to Rebecca. "Thank you for your kind offer."

"Very good, Mr. Southall," replied Colonel Porterfield as he took the letter. "Captain Drew is expecting you. He is a good man and will take care of you."

John bowed and departed to look for Captain Drew. But he was busy tracking down rations for the company when John found him, so he waved John off to Sergeant Palmer.

"Find a musket and cartridge box for this lad, sergeant. He's Captain Southall's boy from Williamsburg, and will be with us for a while."

Sergeant Palmer returned with the items. "So, your father is Captain Southall, eh? He's a good man. I always enjoyed my visits to his tavern when I was in Williamsburg."

"Thank you, sergeant," John replied as he took possession of the musket and cartridge box. "Did you visit often?"

"Not very. Usually just once a year when I came to town to sell my tobacco notes." He eyed the scar along John's arm. "I'm told you were with Buford in South Carolina?" Sergeant Palmer ventured.

"Yes," John sighed. "It didn't go well. British cavalry caught us while we were marching back."

"I've heard," replied the sergeant. "Most of Buford's men were captured, a lot killed. You were one of the lucky ones, escaping like that."

John wondered if the sergeant was questioning his courage with the last comment and looked intently at him, the words drying on his tongue. How does someone apologize for being alive?

The sergeant seemed to understand and gave him a sad smile. "There's no shame in surviving, lad," he said. "The important thing is that you've lived to fight another day—

and fight we will." He patted John on the shoulder and then walked away.

On the afternoon of June 30th, the troops were ordered to cook their meager rations and prepare to march in the morning.

To John's surprise, Abigail—accompanied by her father—visited the camp that same evening. "Going back to war are you, Mr. Southall?" she smirked, one hand on her hip.

"I'll try not to get wounded and create more work for you, Miss Jenkins," John grinned.

Abigail laughed, her eyes sparkling. "Good. Because I meant what I said earlier—you *are* a lot of work." She drew closer to him and reached for his arm. "But you've healed quite nicely," she said as she inspected him. "Your scars are barely noticeable."

"I will always be indebted to you," John said. Then he surprised her—and himself. "May I write to you?" he asked.

Abigail dropped his arm and blushed. "Of course—if you ever get the chance. I will always welcome a letter from you." She paused and bit her lower lip. "But only if it's good news."

John laughed. "I will write nothing but," he said as he bowed to her.

Abigail curtsied in response and then walked to her father and took his arm. "Shall we proceed, Father?" The two turned to leave and Abigail chanced one last look over her shoulder—John was still watching her, beaming. She whipped her head forward, fighting to suppress her own smile.

Chapter Thirteen

Battle of Camden

August 1780

The American troops that marched from Hillsborough were commanded by General Johann de Kalb, a French volunteer who had joined the American cause in 1777. General Washington sent de Kalb south with over a thousand troops from the main army in the spring of 1780. They were Continentals from Maryland and Delaware.

The troops joined Colonel Porterfield's detachment at Hillsborough in late June and General de Kalb led the entire force of fifteen hundred men south on July 1st, to challenge the British. They had marched for just five days, however, when a shortage of food forced them to halt. They spent much of their time gathering food while they were stuck in central North Carolina. John was grateful for the pause, and took the opportunity to write to Abigail.

July 7, 1780

Dear Miss Jenkins,

We have been stuck on the bank of the Deep River because we have run out of food. When we left Hillsborough, Colonel Porterfield had four hundred men, but we will soon be down to one hundred because most have finished their term of service and are to return home. One of those lucky men will deliver this to you on his way through Hillsborough.

We have had a hard time of things, and spend most of our time looking for food, but there is not enough to be found. We may have to turn back if we don't find enough soon. I confess that I hope this is the case, for I would like to see you again.

Please give my regards to your father. I wish you good health and remain,

Your Most Humble and Obedient Servant,

John Southall

General Horatio Gates, the victor of Saratoga, assumed command of the army while they were stuck on the Deep River. Gates had fallen out of favor with Congress two years earlier during the Valley Forge encampment when he supported a plot to replace General Washington as commander-in-chief. Congress had stuck with Washington and Gates had left the army, but when things turned sour in the South in 1780, Congress asked General Gates to return and rebuild the Southern Army.

Gates attached some militia and cavalry under a French officer, Lieutenant Colonel Charles Armand, to Portfield's command, which brought his force back up to four hundred.

John and the others in Porterfield's detachment were the advance guard of the army and they led the march south when General Gates finally resumed his advance in early August. Nearly two thousand militia had joined General Gates at this time from Virginia and North Carolina, which increased his entire force to three thousand men.

The British Army had extended its control into the middle of South Carolina after Charleston surrendered in May. And to maintain this control, they had created a chain of fortified towns. Camden was one such town and General Gates hoped to capture it from the British.

The American army, still low on food, marched slowly toward Camden in August. Living mostly on green corn, apples, and peaches that they picked from the farms they passed, it was a hungry and sickly American army that halted just thirteen miles from Camden on August 14th.

General Gates did not plan to attack Camden directly. Instead, he sought to defend a strong position outside of town and wait for the British to attack. This tactic had worked well for Gates at Saratoga, and he hoped it would work again at Camden.

Informed by scouts that a strong, defensible position was just a few miles ahead, Gates ordered a night march and sent Colonel Porterfield's detachment ahead to lead the way. They began their march at 10 p.m., followed by the rest of the army about a half hour later.

Porterfield's cavalry—some sixty strong—led the American column along the sandy, moonlit road toward Camden. To the left of the cavalry were North Carolina militia under Major John Armstrong. They marched in single file, parallel with the road and cavalry, about twenty-five yards off the dirt road in open woods.

To the right of the road, also twenty-five yards into the woods, marched John in similar fashion with Colonel Porterfield's Virginians. Porterfield was on horseback at the head of his Virginians and commanded the entire force.

John was in the lead company of the column, only about thirty yards behind Porterfield.

The light of a full moon reflected off the sandy white ground, making it appear almost daylight. John and his comrades marched in strict silence—unaware that General Charles Cornwallis and two thousand British troops were marching straight at them. Cornwallis had hoped to surprise the Americans at dawn, but instead, both armies were surprised when their advance guards collided into each other sometime after midnight.

Lieutenant Colonel Banastre Tarleton and his British Legion of cavalry and infantry led the British Army. These were the same men who had wiped out Colonel Buford's Virginians at Waxhaws. They no doubt expected a similar outcome again.

A lone American horseman riding about three hundred yards ahead of Colonel Armand's cavalry spotted Tarleton's approach and fired a warning shot from his pistol.

John heard the shot somewhere ahead and froze with the rest of the column, his heart thumping and hands tight on his musket. He strained his eyes toward the road to see what was happening, then heard the pounding hooves of a single horse riding hard toward them—the lone horseman that had been in advance of the column. *He saw something,* thought John, *but what*?

The rider, clearly agitated, pulled up to Colonel Armand at the head of the cavalry. John and the others around him struggled to listen but could not hear what he said. Colonel Armand suddenly spurred his horse and galloped toward Colonel Porterfield.

Leaning over his saddle, Armand whispered to Colonel Porterfield. "There is the enemy, sir. Shall I charge them?"

"By all means, sir," Porterfield replied and Armand rushed back to his cavalry waiting in the road.

John, of course, did not hear any of this, but he could tell that something significant was afoot. Just as Armand reached his cavalry, a blast of a French horn from Tarleton's Legion—followed by yells of "charge, charge, charge!"—filled the air. Tarleton's cavalry had crept up on the Americans and attacked!

Some of Armand's horsemen immediately fled, but others remained with him and fought Tarleton and his men with saber and pistol.

John heard Colonel Porterfield call out, "Infantry advance at the trot," and they all moved forward, still parallel with the road and the clashing cavalry on it. They had advanced only about thirty yards when Porterfield ordered, "Halt, face to the road, fire!"

John did as he was told, firing at shadows of horses and men just twenty-five yards in front of him. He was momentarily blinded by the flash of his musket and the blasts of those around him, but he immediately reached back to his cartridge box and grabbed another cartridge to reload.

Tarleton and his cavalry, thinking they had easily overwhelmed the Americans, were shocked to find enemy infantry on their flank at point blank range. They wheeled their horses around and retreated in disarray.

John had reloaded in twenty seconds, but he could see no targets to aim at and did not want to accidently shoot any American cavalry, so he held his fire.

But then he noticed dark figures on foot scurrying on the road, passing them in the opposite direction. *They're surrounding us,* he realized. Then he heard the booming voice of Colonel Porterfield.

“Fire, lads! Fire!” Porterfield yelled, and John leveled his musket toward the dark figures in the road and fired. As John furiously reloaded, he noticed that the movement to his front had halted, then bright flashes erupted in front of him accompanied by a roar of musketry.

He ducked down instinctively as musket balls whizzed over his head. He could hear them strike branches and trees and he prayed, *Lord, don’t let one hit me*.

He sprung up, rammed his cartridge down, and fired his third shot, not bothering to wait for an order. He repeated the process again, intensely focused on this one task—load and fire, load and fire. After his next shot, however, he heard someone to his left cry out, “They’re flanking us!”

Muskets flashed again and musket balls flew at them from two directions now, John’s front and left. He looked frantically to his right to Colonel Porterfield, hoping for some direction, but the colonel lurched abruptly forward in his saddle. Something had struck him in the leg. Porterfield, holding the neck of his horse to steady himself, said something to Captain Drew, who was standing next to him. The captain then turned down the line and shouted, “Withdraw! Withdraw!”

John turned to flee, but stopped. *That was a musket ball that hit his leg,* he thought. *Colonel Porterfield needs help.* He ran to Captain Drew and another officer attending to Porterfield. The colonel remained in his saddle, but just barely, holding tight to the mane of his horse to steady himself. But then an enemy volley just thirty yards away spooked Porterfield's horse, which reared and threw him off.

He landed hard on the ground, his wounded leg turned back under him. John was horrified at the wound; his shin was shattered just below the knee and the colonel bled profusely. *My God, how can he stand it?* thought John.

Captain Drew had disappeared but the other officer, Captain Guilford Dudley with the North Carolina militia, was still there and together they—with the help of a third soldier—lifted Colonel Porterfield upon Captain Dudley's horse. Dudley then jumped on and tried to hold Porterfield up while John and the other soldier turned the horse to the rear and walked alongside to keep the colonel from falling off.

John noticed that blood had filled Colonel Porterfield's boot and that his torn leg swung limply back and forth, apparently disconnected from the shattered bone.

They traveled just sixty yards deeper into the woods when Colonel Porterfield fainted from loss of blood and began to slip off the horse. John caught him and lowered him to the ground and after a moment the colonel came to.

Seemingly resigned to his fate, he urged John and the others to leave him. They refused and lifted him back upon the horse. When they reached a thicket of persimmon bushes, they stopped and lowered him to the ground while Captain Dudley formed a splint from branches to place on the colonel's leg. John's blanket was cut into several long strips and then bound tightly around the improvised splint and shattered leg.

Thankfully, this slowed his blood loss and revived Colonel Porterfield, who was placed back upon the horse. The men continued on at an angle away from the road, but toward the American army, for a mile or so until they reached the edge of a swamp.

They lowered Colonel Porterfield to the ground to rest under a tree. Captain Dudley instructed John and the other soldier to go and find the army and bring back a surgeon and several men to tend to the colonel.

They did as they were told.

"Did you see his wound?" asked the soldier running with John. "It's horrible."

"I know. It's a miracle he's still alive."

"He'll lose the leg for sure," the soldier shook his head sadly. "And probably his life, too."

John said nothing but ran a little faster. They found the American army stopped and deployed for battle. In the dim light of pre-dawn, a sentry called out to them to halt. They did so and yelled they needed help for Colonel Porterfield.

Captain Drew was nearby and heard them. "Southall, is that you?" he yelled. "Hold your fire sentinel, he's ours."

John rushed up to Captain Drew. "Sir, Colonel Porterfield needs help. He needs a surgeon for his leg. He's with an officer near a swamp, and we're to take a surgeon and some men back to them."

"Sergeant Adams!" yelled Captain Drew. "Find Dr. Griffith and bring him and four men to me now! Tell the doctor to bring his bag."

John and the other soldier led the party back to Colonel Porterfield. "Well done, well done, lads," said Captain Dudley, relieved that they had actually returned.

Doctor Griffith tended to the colonel's leg while John and the others made a litter from branches and blankets to carry the colonel.

With the gray of dawn appearing on the horizon, the rescue party proceeded with Colonel Porterfield. They did not return to the army, but instead to a house half a mile away along the edge of the swamp.

They brought Colonel Porterfield inside and laid him on a bed. The lady of the house brought a pitcher of water, followed by an enslaved women with a basin full of water. Doctor Griffith said something to Captain Drew, who then turned to John. "You've done all you can, lads. Best to return to the army with me now."

Two of the other men stayed behind to assist the doctor, who was preparing to amputate the colonel's leg when they left.

Off in the distance they could hear cannon fire. The sun had been up for nearly an hour and a battle was raging just a mile away.

"Come, let's see what all the fuss is about," said Captain Drew.

As they made their way to the battle, they noticed men—many men—running away from it.

"I think those are General Stevens' men," said Captain Drew with concern. Stevens had joined the army just a week before with seven hundred Virginia militia. "This doesn't look good."

As they went a little further, they encountered a Continental officer with blood splattered on his face. Captain Drew stopped him and learned that the battle was lost; the left wing of the army—where the Virginia militia was posted—had fled at the start of the battle.

"The Continentals held as long as they could," said the bloodied officer. "De Kalb fought like a giant, but the enemy gained our rear and surrounded us, so we had to flee."

"Are you all right, Lieutenant?" asked Captain Drew, referring to the blood on his face.

"Yes, I'm fine," said the Lieutenant as he wiped at the smears. "The blood isn't mine."

"Where are you off to?" Captain Drew asked.

"I'm not sure. Everyone is heading north, but I'm not sure where."

John listened to the discussion with a sinking heart. They had been defeated in battle again—and days of long marches to safety undoubtedly lay ahead.

“Let’s go, lads,” said Captain Drew. “Let’s find the army.”

Chapter Fourteen

Back to Hillsborough

Fall 1780

John headed north with Captain Drew and the remnants of the army and reached Charlotte in five days. Several hundred battered Continentals joined them there.

Unlike the militia on the left wing of the army, General de Kalb's Maryland and Delaware Continentals had fought heroically at Camden—their commander especially so. Outnumbered and overwhelmed by the British they had stood for as long as they could, but ultimately broke and were forced to retreat before the British encircled them completely.

General de Kalb had remained behind, mortally wounded. Nearly a thousand Americans—mostly Continentals—had been killed, wounded, or captured in the battle as well. It was a decisive defeat, but hundreds of Continentals managed to escape and flee north, preserving a core of troops from which to rebuild the Southern army.

Although two-thirds of the American army that had marched to Camden had comprised of militia, few of those troops withdrew to Charlotte. Most headed for their homes instead, finished with war.

Captain Drew and John located the remnants of their company— which had gotten swept up in the panic of the militia—in Charlotte, and fell in with them as everyone marched north. It took two weeks to reach Hillsborough, but John was pleased to be back—in part because of his ensured safety, but also because his return gave him a chance to see Abigail again.

General Gates had arrived in Hillsborough by horse more than a week earlier—well ahead of his troops—and many of his men ridiculed him for what seemed to them his cowardly flight from Camden. He claimed he tried to rally the militia when they broke, but had gotten caught up in their retreat. Most of the Continentals, however, didn't believe him. They thought he had outright abandoned them to their fate as soon as the militia broke.

John wasn't sure what to think, and frankly, didn't care. He was just glad to be back in Hillsborough—alive and unhurt, and eager to see Abigail. She seemed pleased to see him, but their first visit was brief due to the sheer amount of wounded.

"I'm so relieved to see you, John," Abigail said when he entered the makeshift hospital in Hillsborough. She eyed the length of him. "You kept your word, I see," she grinned.

John returned the smile. "I learned my lesson the first time and kept away from slashing sabers."

"I would like to hear all about it," said Abigail as she unwrapped the bandaged arm of a soldier to check for infection. "But as you can see, we're quite busy. Where are you posted?"

"I'm not sure. Somewhere in town, but Captain Drew hasn't said where yet."

"Well, I suggest you go and find your captain, and when you learn where you are quartered, let me know. I won't be going anywhere for a while." She then redirected her attention to the wounded soldier and examined the unwrapped arm. "That looks to be healing nicely," she said. "You are fortunate it did not strike the bone."

John felt an urge to stay and watch Abigail, to help if he could, but he knew he'd only get in the way. He bid her farewell and went off to find Captain Drew.

When he had finally tracked the captain down, he was told the company would bed down under the stars on the west side of town. Feeling more settled now that he knew where he'd be sleeping, he reached for his journal and pencils in his pack and sat down to write to James.

September 3, 1780

Dear James,

Before this letter reaches you, you will have likely heard of yet another defeat in South Carolina near a place called Camden. Everyone blames the Virginia militia for the defeat. They broke and ran at the start of the battle without firing a shot.

I was not actually in this fight; my fight occurred a few hours before. I was with Colonel Porterfield's advance guard on a night march toward Camden when we collided with the enemy. They were the same troops who defeated us at Waxhaws.

They surprised our cavalry in the road, but we surprised them from the woods, and for a moment it seemed we had them beat, for they rode off in disarray.

The fight had only begun, however, for then several hundred infantry arrived. We surprised them with a volley at point blank range from the woods, but they recovered and fought back.

Colonel Porterfield was on his horse when a musket ball struck his shin bone and nearly took his leg off. With our line crumbling, he ordered a withdrawal, but was so weak from the loss of blood that he fell from his horse.

I witnessed all of this and offered my assistance, which was readily accepted. An officer from North Carolina and a soldier from Virginia stayed with Colonel Porterfield, and we managed to move him out of danger.

His wound was grievous though, and he passed out several times. After we had gone about a mile, we stopped to rest and then I and the other soldier were sent to get help. We returned with a surgeon and several other men and took Colonel Porterfield to a nearby house, then tried to rejoin our unit. But the battle was already over and lost and all was in chaos.

We found the army fleeing north and went with them until we reached this place, Hillsborough. It's a shattered and demoralized force that camps here this evening, and I doubt we are capable of any resistance should the enemy push us. We are told reinforcements are coming from

Virginia, but we've been told that for weeks and none have arrived.

There is one good thing about being back in Hillsborough though. It allows me to become better acquainted with a young lady. Her name is Abigail Jenkins. She is the daughter of a local doctor who cared for me when I was sick with the pox. I find myself uncommonly fond of her, perhaps because she saved my life, and am eager to spend more time with her.

I hope all is well with you and the Nelsons. Please give my love to our parents and siblings and to Rebecca. Until we meet again, please remember that I remain,

Your Obedient and Loving Brother,

John

With his letter completed, John stretched out on the ground under a tree and succumbed to sleep. He was not asleep for long, however, and awoke with a start to find Abigail crouching over him, her green eyes glistening.

"Napping on duty, eh?" she tutted. "I ought to report you."

"I just dozed off a second ago," he said as he ran a hand through his hair in an attempt to smooth it. It was always a mess when he woke up.

"Well, then I guess I can overlook it," she smiled. "It would not do, after all, for my father and I to dine with a soldier facing court martial."

John stared up at Abigail confused.

"I'm here to invite you to dine with us tomorrow, silly," Abigail clarified. "That is, *if* you don't have any napping duty."

John laughed. "I would be honored to dine with you, but I just realized I don't know where you live."

"Well, that's easy to fix. Look over there." She pointed to a two-story brick home just a hundred yards away. "My home and my father's office."

"Very good," replied James, rising to his feet and brushing himself off. "What time shall I arrive?"

"We dine at three every day."

"Then I shall arrive by two thirty."

"Very good. My father will be pleased."

Neither knew what to say next so an awkward pause ensued, but to John's relief Abigail broke it with an observation.

"You really need some knew shoes, soldier," she said looking down at his feet. "Perhaps I can find you a pair that fit."

"I would surely welcome a new pair."

Abigail stared at him, and John knew she was waiting for him to say more, but his mind was a hopeless blank. *Say something you idiot*, he thought, but nothing came.

Abigail clasped her hands behind her and swayed. "Well, then that will be my mission, to find you a new pair of shoes. They likely won't be newly made, but they will be new to you."

John smiled. "You're too kind to me."

"I'm kind to everyone, Mr. Southall. But now I must be off to start my mission. If you'll excuse me." She turned to go, throwing a smile over her shoulder.

"Thank you, Abigail. I shall see you tomorrow," John called after her.

"It is my pleasure, John. Just don't make me regret it by napping on duty anymore!"

John arrived early for dinner the next day, and shared his experiences at Camden with Doctor Jenkins and Abigail.

It had been a long time since he had had such a dinner, and he took full advantage of the opportunity.

"Beats your rations in camp I imagine," chuckled the doctor, as John took a second portion of pie.

"Indeed, it does, sir," replied John, a bit concerned that he looked like a glutton—but not concerned enough to stop himself from having seconds.

After dinner, the trio retired to the front porch and chatted about Hillsborough and Williamsburg. The doctor excused himself after a half hour, however, explaining that he had some work to do inside.

John and Abigail were left alone on the porch, sitting next to each other on a bench.

Abigail had carried the majority of their conversations thus far, and so John expected her to continue to do so, but she sat uncharacteristically quiet next to him, swinging her feet gently, her hands in her lap.

"So," John started, hoping she'd speak up. But Abigail only turned to look at him expectantly. He studied her face as she stared, mapping the small collection of freckles across her cheeks, the high arch of her eyebrows. *They're raised that way because she is waiting for you to say something!* his inner-voice chastised. John swallowed.

"Medicine," he blurted. "How do you know so much about medicine?"

A single brow arched even higher. "My father?"

John flushed. *You idiot,* he thought. *Why are you so bad at this?*

But Abigail laughed and patted his arm, leaning closer to him. "Ask me if I enjoy it," she whispered.

"Do you enjoy it?" John said in a rush.

Abigail lit up. "Oh, yes! It's not easy work, but it makes me feel," she paused, "powerful. Putting people back together."

John blanched, remembering the pile of limbs he'd seen before. "You're stronger than I am," he said. "Being around all that blood?" he shivered.

Abigail laughed. "But you're a soldier! Certainly you've seen your fair share of blood?"

"Oh, I have," John grimaced. "And it was terrible. But I imagine nothing like what you see regularly."

Abigail looked off into the distance, her eyes focused on something John couldn't see. "It can be terrible," she said softly. "But it is very rewarding work." She turned back to John, her smile returned. "Many men struggle to feel like themselves after they've been wounded—

especially if they've suffered an amputation. It's a great change, learning to live without a part of you you've had forever. I help heal their physical wounds, but I like to think I help them in another way, too. By guiding them toward acceptance. To adapt. Just because it's different doesn't mean it's bad."

John wasn't sure what to say. "That's…" he sputtered, running his hand through his hair, wracking his brain for a response. "Indeed."

"I suffered a bad fall from a horse when I was a child," Abigail said. "My father is an excellent doctor, but it was a bad break, broken in multiple places. It never healed quite right so," she paused to stand. "I don't move very gracefully," she took a few steps forward, and John noticed for the first time a slight limp.

"I-I never noticed," he said.

"Most don't," she shrugged. "I've had years of practice, so I hide it well. But when I was younger, I had to use crutches to get around. Adapt." She sat back down next to John, her body just ever so slightly closer now.

"Does it still cause you pain?" John asked.

"Only when it rains," Abigail replied. "Or when I overexert myself. Don't ever ask me to a race," she laughed. “I’m fiercely competitive and forget my shortcomings.”

John smiled. “I wouldn’t call that a shortcoming.” He reached for her hand, threaded his fingers through hers and squeezed. “Just another one of your strengths.”

Abigail stared at his hand on hers for a moment before beaming up at him.

John was invited to dine with the Jenkins again a few days later, and he gladly accepted. At the end of dinner, Abigail mentioned how busy things had gotten in the hospital.

John immediately volunteered to help. “I can talk to Captain Drew and see if he might spare me. There really isn’t much to do in camp.”

Abigail looked at her father, who smiled at her and nodded. “That would be grand, Mr. Southall,” she said. “We accept any help you can offer.”

John reported to the hospital two days later, ready to pitch in. The hospital was full with sick and wounded soldiers from Camden, and every day a few more arrived.

“Find a couple of men to help you set up some shelter alongside the building,” instructed Doctor Jenkins. “We’ll put those who are out of danger there for the time being.”

John and several other men set up numerous brush arbors and put cots under them for patients to lie on. It was still warm in North Carolina, so the cots had to be moved multiple times a day to remain in the shade as the sun shifted west.

John was also tasked to tend several fires over which kettles of water boiled, and late in the afternoon he helped feed some of the most severely hurt soldiers.

Although he was kept busy at the hospital, he managed to spend a surprising amount of time with Abigail, who was constantly running about checking on patients and changing bandages.

"Mr. Southall, can you spare a moment?" was heard several times each hour as Abigail called him for assistance. Each time he would drop what he was doing and go to her—usually to help move a patient who was too weak to move himself.

"Thank you, sir," was her usual response, but her smile displayed much more than her formal gratitude.

Although they rarely found time to talk privately, John enjoyed being at the hospital. He was amazed at Abigail's constant poise; nothing ever fazed her.

She's something else, he thought as he watched her move expertly from patient to patient.

John settled into a daily routine that continued for nearly a week. It was interrupted, however, by the arrival of Colonel Buford and his three hundred and fifty Virginia Continentals.

"I'm afraid I can't help any longer, Abby," John said to her quietly the day Buford arrived. "I'll likely have to fall in with Colonel Buford's troops."

"Of course," Abigail replied. "He should know though that you have been a big help."

John reported to Colonel Buford in the afternoon and was greeted enthusiastically.

"Mr. Southall, you look all mended and recovered. Ready to rejoin the battalion?"

"I am, sir."

"Good! You'll be assigned to Captain Wallace's company. I believe you were in his brother's company before…." the colonel couldn't bring himself to say Waxhaws.

"I was, sir."

"Excellent. You will find that they are cut from the same cloth. Go and report to him."

John departed and found Captain Wallace. Captain Wallace was older than his brother Adam—John's former company commander—but the resemblance was clear.

"Sir, I am to join your company. My name is John Southall."

"Southall, aye, I've heard of you. Something about helping Colonel Porterfield from the field at Camden."

"Yes, sir, that was I. I'm afraid he was still captured though."

"Aye, but he survived, son. He's a prisoner in Camden recovering from his wound. We received word from him the other day. Although the ghastly wound took his leg, it didn't take his life—thanks to you. Well done."

John tried his best to hide a smile. "Thank you, sir."

"How did you come to serve with Porterfield if you're a Continental?" the captain asked.

"After our defeat in May, I was brought here, wounded and sick with smallpox. By the time I recovered, Colonel Buford had marched back to Virginia, so Colonel Porterfield asked me to serve under him instead."

Captain Wallace nodded in understanding. "Whose company were you in at Waxhaws?"

John hesitated a moment before answering. "Your brother's, sir," he gulped. "He was a fine officer."

Captain Wallace nodded again, staring off in the distance—no doubt thinking of his brother. He redirected his gaze to John, his eyes softer. "Well, I hope you find me equally worthy, Mr. Southall. Go and report to Lieutenant Ball. He'll know best where to place you in the company."

John was placed in the first platoon, in the second rank—his usual position because of his height.

"How are you situated for a weapon and clothing?" Lieutenant Ball asked.

"I have everything I need, sir. Except proper shoes, and perhaps another shirt."

"Yes, you plainly need better shoes," laughed Lieutenant Ball as he looked down at John's battered pair. "I'll see what I can do. But for now, get your gear and report back to me. We brought tents with us from Chesterfield and I need to find a place for you in one."

John stopped to visit with Abigail before returning to his new company. "It looks like I'll be posted over there," he said, pointing off in the distance. "I'll try to visit as often as I can."

"I hope so," Abigail grinned.

John was assigned to a tent with five other soldiers. It was a tight fit, but the weather was finally beginning to cool, so the tight quarters kept the soldiers warmer than if they had been lying out under the stars.

On his third day back with his unit, John was summoned by Colonel Buford. When he reported, he was surprised to find Doctor Jenkins with the colonel.

"Mr. Southall, Doctor Jenkins tells me you performed excellent service in the hospital prior to our arrival. He'd like you to return for as long as we are here. Do you have any objections?"

"Certainly not, sir," replied John, happy for the chance to return.

"Good, then off with you. I'll inform Captain Wallace that you've been detached to the hospital."

John and Doctor Jenkins walked back to the hospital together. "Thank you, sir, for arranging this," John said.

Doctor Jenkins looked up at John and smiled. "It's not me you should thank, son. Abigail insisted that the hospital suffered from your absence, and she kept on me about it until I agreed to bring you back. She's a persistent one, my daughter."

John chuckled, "That she is, sir," and kept walking. When they entered the hospital, they were greeted by Abigail.

"Thank God! We have more help with the chamber pots!" she declared with a smile. "Here, these are for you," she continued, handing John a pair of slightly worn shoes.

John smiled and bowed in response. "A pleasure to see you again, Miss Jenkins. Happy to be of service. And thank you for the shoes.

In early October a new officer arrived in camp. Colonel Daniel Morgan, soon to be promoted to brigadier-general, was famous throughout the army for his exploits in Boston, Quebec, and Saratoga. He had risen quickly through the officer ranks because of his meritorious service, but when he was denied the honor of commanding a new corps of Light Infantry in 1779, he left the army in protest. Convinced by General Gates to return, however, he joined the Southern army in Hillsborough.

Morgan was a giant of a man, over six feet tall and solid. He had a scar on his cheek from a gunshot during the French and Indian War, and scars on his back from nearly five hundred lashes he'd received for insubordination toward a British officer in the same conflict.

He had escaped harm thus far in the current war, but had been captured with Colonel Porterfield at Quebec and was held captive for seven months.

John was excited about Morgan's arrival—and even more excited to learn that Captain Wallace's company had been attached to Morgan's command. Colonel Morgan was to lead the army's light corps, made up of over two hundred of the best troops in the army.

John's enthusiasm for the assignment dimmed, however, when he was ordered back to his unit to prepare to march. Morgan's light corps was to march to Salisbury—and that meant he had to say goodbye to Abigail.

Over the course of the last six weeks, John had grown exceedingly fond of Abigail. He believed her feelings for him were just as strong, and this was confirmed when he informed her of his imminent departure.

"I hate that you have to go," Abigail murmured against his chest as they embraced in a quiet corner of the hospital.

"As do I," John said, tightening his arms around her.

John and the light corps marched out of camp in mid-October. When they arrived in Salisbury, one hundred miles away, they learned stunning news. One thousand militia from the western frontier had destroyed an equal number of troops from General Cornwallis's army at a place called King's Mountain.

The surprising defeat of the British troops that were to guard Cornwallis's left flank on his march into North Carolina, prompted him to postpone his planned invasion there and withdraw to South Carolina for the winter.

General Morgan, who received his promotion to brigadier-general while on the march, moved his light corps further south, past Charlotte and encamped near the South Carolina border. They remained there for six weeks, protecting the rest of the army which had marched to Charlotte with General Gates.

John wrote two letters to Abigail during this time, but received none from her, which discouraged him greatly. *Maybe she hasn't received my letters,* he thought. *Or maybe she just doesn't care. Maybe I misunderstood her.* The uncertainty plagued him daily, and it was with much relief that he finally received a letter from her at the end of November.

November 5, 1780

Dearest John,

It has been nearly a month since you left and I have yet to hear from you. This is my second letter. I can only assume the first has yet to reach you.

General Gates is preparing to march to join you, and a kind officer has offered to carry this letter to Captain Wallace to give to you.

We heard the happy news of King's Mountain and hope that means the British will leave us alone. It seems they may be more interested in Virginia now, for a report arrived yesterday that a British squadron had appeared there. I hope your family and friends remain safe.

We have somehow struggled on at the hospital without you, though nobody empties the chamber pots as well as you. It's pretty quiet here now, many of those who were with us when you were here have returned to the army or returned to their homes. Too many have sadly passed.

I pray every day that you return safely, for I miss you so. Please stay safe and well, and write as soon as you can. Your Ever Affectionate Friend, and Nurse,

Abigail

John was beaming when he finished the letter. *She does like me,* he thought. *How did I get so lucky?*

Chapter Fifteen

Virginia is Alarmed

Fall 1780

The summer had been much less eventful in Virginia than it had been in the Carolinas. The most exciting event that James experienced, indirectly, was the birth of the Nelson's tenth child in early October. They named her Susanna. Her arrival was a bit disruptive to James's daily routine, but he adjusted and continued to teach the Nelson children.

The joy produced by a new baby was tempered, however, on the morning of October 21st, when General Nelson received alarming news that a powerful British fleet of sixty ships had sailed into Hampton Roads and landed troops. He immediately wrote to Governor Jefferson with the news and urged him to order militia from the middle of the state to march to Williamsburg, where he would take command of them.

Because James served in the militia, he should have reported to Captain Gibbon's Yorktown company when

General Nelson ordered the militia out, but the general had other plans for him.

"I need a good aide-de-camp, Mr. Southall, and can think of no one better than yourself. Will you serve as my aide?"

James was stunned and honored by the request. *Me? But I have little military experience or knowledge, why me?* he wondered while the general waited for an answer.

"I am honored, sir, but do you really think I am well suited for the responsibility?"

"As I said, I can think of none better than yourself. I need someone I can depend on, and you have more than proven yourself these past months with my family."

James smiled and bowed in appreciation. "I would be honored to serve as your aide, sir."

"Very well then," General Nelson said with a smile. "Of course, we can't have you as a private in such a position. So, you shall now be Lieutenant Southall."

General Nelson led James into his study and motioned for him to sit at a table. The general himself sat at his desk.

"Your duties will vary as my aide, but one thing you can expect is to write a lot of letters on my behalf. And you start right now. I need you to write to General Weedon and General Muhlenberg."

General George Weedon was a former officer in the Continental Army who had resigned because of a dispute over rank. Still, his experience in the New York Campaign and Battle of Trenton in 1776, as well as the battles of Brandywine and Germantown in 1777, made him a valuable commander for Virginia's militia.

General Peter Muhlenberg was still a general in the Continental Army, posted at Chesterfield Courthouse. He had struggled for months to raise, outfit, and train new Virginians for the Southern army, but only had eight hundred poorly clad troops with him when the British arrived in November. General Nelson wanted Muhlenberg to march as many of his Continentals as he could to Williamsburg, and he wanted Weedon, who was in Fredericksburg, to march to Richmond.

"Start each letter with an introduction of yourself as my aide, and explain that you are writing on my behalf," General Nelson said. "Then write that a British force of sixty ships has been sighted in Hampton Roads and has landed troops at Portsmouth. Tell them the militia has been called out in this region and is gathering in Williamsburg.

I intend to send a large detachment to Hampton tomorrow, but cannot cross the river to the southside until reinforcements arrive. Tell them they are to march with as many men as they can to Williamsburg and Richmond, and then to await further instructions from either myself or Governor Jefferson. End each letter with the usual niceties."

While James composed the letters, General Nelson wrote orders to the surrounding counties instructing their militia to muster. The militia north of Williamsburg were to march to the former capital, but the militia in Yorktown, Hampton, and Newport News were to stay where they were and await further instructions.

General Nelson finished his orders first and left the room. He returned a minute later with an empty portmanteau and handed it to James.

"Lord knows how long we will be away, so pack it full with clothes and anything else you absolutely need," said the General. "It all has to fit in there though, so be selective."

James dashed upstairs and returned a few minutes later with a full portmanteau. The Nelson children were gathered in the central passage; they had heard the news of

James's appointment and congratulated Lieutenant Southall.

"Have Joseph saddle up Spartan for Lieutenant Southall and secure his baggage," General Nelson said as he turned to an enslaved man. "I shall ride Apollo, and you Buck." He turned back to face James. "Now I must pack," he said before disappearing into his bed chamber.

If only John could see me now, thought James. *From private to lieutenant in the blink of an eye. And my own mount too*!

General Nelson and James, accompanied by the general's personal servant, Samuel, set off for Williamsburg just after noon.

They rode hard and as they approached the city, they could hear the bell of Bruton Church ringing an alarm. The messenger who had informed the General about the British earlier in the day had continued to Williamsburg—per Nelson's instructions—to warn the city.

The small party rode down Duke of Gloucester Street, past the Raleigh Tavern to the Powder Magazine, where militia from the city were gathering. James's father, who had risen to the rank of militia colonel, was the ranking officer in attendance and was busy organizing the troops when James and General Nelson arrived.

"General Nelson, sir," Colonel Southall said when he noticed him approach, still on his horse.

"Colonel, sir, allow me to present Lieutenant Southall. I believe you two are acquainted," said the general with a grin.

James smiled at his father, who stood confused and speechless.

"I needed an aide and could think of none better than your son."

James's father snapped back to attention and nodded in agreement. "Yes, sir, General. I think James will make a fine aide. He's always been a clever one, and you'll not find a more responsible lad errr… officer, in the militia."

James reddened, embarrassed at the attention, but was happy that his father was so pleased by his appointment.

"So, what is the situation here, Colonel?" asked General Nelson as he dismounted.

"The city militia is forming, sir. And riders have spread the call for neighboring counties to send their militia here."

"Very good, Colonel. The alarm should reach Richmond by tomorrow morning, so it is likely we will not hear from the Governor for two days. In the meantime, we need to prepare for every possibility."

General Nelson and Colonel Southall walked into the Guardhouse next to the Powder Magazine. James followed behind. The officers agreed that there would be no movement from Williamsburg until the morning, but it was likely Colonel Southall would have to lead troops to Hampton in case the British landed there.

General Nelson met with Colonel Southall for nearly two hours. James stood in the doorway as a gatekeeper, shielding the officers from unnecessary distraction while he listened to their discussion. Both men were concerned about something that had long plagued Virginia's forces—a shortage of muskets and ammunition.

A little after 6 p.m., General Nelson announced that he was famished and asked Colonel Southall if he might still procure a meal at the Raleigh.

"Of course, General, anything you want. And we have several bedchambers available as well."

General Nelson asked James to fetch Captain Davenport. When he arrived, Nelson asked him, "have you had dinner yet, Captain?"

"Yes, sir, I have," replied Davenport.

"Excellent! Then you are to remain here until I or Colonel Southall returns. Keep whatever men you need here and dismiss the rest to their homes—but warn them to be ready to form at a moment's notice. Direct any troops who need shelter to stay in the barracks behind the palace, and send an officer or two there to supervise." The General returned his focus to Colonel Southall. "Colonel, shall we proceed to the Raleigh?"

When they entered the front door of the Raleigh, Mrs. Southall and her children were there waiting for James. Word had spread back to the tavern that he was in town with General Nelson. They made a big fuss over him and were thrilled by the news of his new position.

He'll be less likely to be in harm's way, thought Mrs. Southall. *Thank God for that.*

James joined his father and General Nelson for dinner in one of the club rooms. Mrs. Southall and the children had dined hours earlier, so she excused herself and tended to the children. As the officers dined, they speculated on what the sudden appearance of the British meant.

"I expect this force will likely cooperate with General Cornwallis in South Carolina in a move against North Carolina," predicted General Nelson. "There is still plenty of time to undertake a movement there, and perhaps secure North Carolina—or at least a portion of it—before the winter sets in."

Colonel Southall and James nodded in agreement.

"The matter at hand for us," continued Nelson, "is to prevent this new force from succeeding in whatever it seeks to do *and* defend as much of Virginia as we can. And on that note, Colonel," the General nodded to him. "I need you to march the troops that are assembled here to Hampton and guard against an attack there. Let them rest in their beds tonight, but recall them to the Magazine in the morning and lead them and whatever other troops who have come to town to Hampton by noon."

"Yes, sir," replied Colonel Southall.

"I shall wait here for the reinforcements and will likely forward them to you in detachments." Then General Nelson turned to James. "Lieutenant, you are to inform Reverend Bracken this evening that we shall need his bell early tomorrow morning. Then return here."

"Yes, sir," replied James, rising from his seat.

"Colonel, I will remain here, but would like you to return to the Magazine to check on the situation there."

"Of course, General," replied Colonel Southall. "I will accompany my s—Lieutenant Southall."

As father and son walked up Duke of Gloucester Street, both beamed with pride.

"You've done well, son," James's father said. "General Nelson has chosen a fine aide."

"Thank you, sir," replied James. "I was quite surprised by his decision, and I confess I was a bit reluctant. I have little experience after all."

"Nonsense!" his father boomed. "You are immensely qualified and will do fine. I am proud of you, James."

The two separated at the Magazine and James continued to the Minister's residence to deliver his message. His father was still at the Magazine when he returned, so he waited for him so that they could walk back to the Raleigh together.

"How have things been these past months, Father?" James asked, referring to business.

"Not so well I'm afraid," his father sighed. "The move has hurt everyone, and half the taverns have shut down already. We're getting by, but business is much slower."

James nodded. *It isn't likely to ever get better either, with the government moved to Richmond,* he thought.

His father changed the disagreeable subject. "How fares Rebecca and her family?"

"They do well," replied James. "Their tavern is smaller than the one they had here, but they are close to where the Assembly meets and are always busy when the legislature is in session."

"Hmmm," his father rubbed his chin. "Anderson was wise to move to Richmond."

Once at the Raleigh, James reported straight to General Nelson, who had retired to his bedchamber but was still awake, writing at a table.

"Is there anything else for me, sir?" James asked.

"No, Lieutenant. You best turn in. We shall be quite busy tomorrow."

The church bell tolled loudly at 8 a.m., once again alarming the surrounding area. Along with the city militia, there was militia from James City, Charles City, and New Kent Counties. Colonel Southall organized them into one battalion and led them south toward Hampton at noon.

James watched his father lead the column on horseback, father and son nodding to each other as the Colonel passed by.

General Nelson made the abandoned Governor's Palace his headquarters, and as militia from other counties arrived, he had them quarter in the large barracks behind the palace.

James spent the day greeting officers and bringing them to see General Nelson. Sometimes he waited with them in the central passage while the General met with another officer. James thought it was odd to see several stools and a rough table in the parlor of the once grand residence. All the fine furnishings had been moved to Richmond when the capital was transferred in the spring.

"I need accurate information!" grumbled General Nelson at one point during the day as he poured over a map of Virginia. Reports on the number of enemy troops and vessels and where they were landing varied wildly, making it difficult to decide next steps.

The truth, though, was that just two thousand two hundred troops comprised General Alexander Leslie's British expedition to Virginia. His task was to create a diversion in Virginia to assist General Cornwallis's planned movement into North Carolina. General Henry Clinton—the overall British commander in New York—suggested to General Leslie in his instructions that he proceed up the James River to Petersburg and Richmond, and destroy whatever military equipment he might find there.

General Leslie may have intended to do so, but on October 23rd, he landed a large party of troops at Newport News and marched into Hampton unopposed. Colonel Southall had not yet reached Hampton, and when he heard the size of the British force that waited there, he wisely chose to keep his distance.

While the British were in Hampton, they learned that a portion of General Cornwallis's army in the Carolinas—commanded by Colonel Patrick Ferguson—had been destroyed at a place called King's Mountain. Ferguson's force, about one thousand strong, had guarded the left flank of General Cornwallis's army on his march into North Carolina. Ferguson's threats to punish anyone not loyal to the British had provoked a fight with a thousand hardy frontiersmen from the Carolinas and Virginia. They attacked Ferguson and his men in early October on a rugged mountain near the border of North and South Carolina. After a fierce battle in which Ferguson and many of his men were killed, the survivors surrendered, handing the Americans their first victory in the south in many months.

When General Leslie heard this news, he correctly assumed that General Cornwallis would postpone his planned invasion of North Carolina. As a result, Leslie adjusted *his* plans, and withdrew his troops across the James River to Portsmouth, waiting for instructions from Cornwallis.

James and General Nelson had ridden south about eighteen miles to Rich Neck—about half way between Williamsburg and Hampton—when they learned that the British had left Hampton. James was relieved to learn they had done so without a fight; that meant his father was safe.

General Nelson was baffled by the British troop movements, and worried a strike upriver at Williamsburg might be in their plans, so he remained at Rich Neck, just a day's march to either Williamsburg or Hampton.

Colonel Southall was ordered to occupy Hampton with the four hundred militia under his command. General Muhlenberg commanded troops across the James River near Smithfield, and General Weedon was gathering reinforcements in Richmond.

But it turned out that none were needed. General Leslie kept his British troops in Portsmouth until mid-November, waiting for instructions from General Cornwallis. When they finally arrived, Leslie loaded his troops aboard the transports and sailed for South Carolina to reinforce Cornwallis.

James remained in the field with General Nelson for another week until it was certain that the British had left. He arrived back at Yorktown with General Nelson at the end of November, and was able to resume his lessons with the children.

While James returned to his life as a civilian, John was encamped with General Morgan's troops south of Charlotte, North Carolina, watching for the British. In early December, General Nathanael Greene of Rhode Island arrived to take over for General Gates and command the American Southern army, per the wishes of Congress and General Washington. Greene was an experienced officer with a solid reputation who had been with the Continental army since the start of the war, but he had never held a separate command before and was thus, unproven. General Gates returned to Virginia, disgraced by his cowardly conduct at Camden.

John knew little about General Greene, but hoped he could stir the army into action. Little had been achieved, or even attempted, since the summer. And with winter settling in, John feared a difficult season ahead. His instincts were, unfortunately, correct—but it would not be in camp where the difficulty lay but rather, in the field.

General Greene worked hard to organize and supply the army, but within two weeks he realized that the region around Charlotte could not adequately supply food for his troops. As a result, he decided to split the army. Greene ordered the bulk of his men to march east with him along the Pee Dee River—about one hundred and twenty-five miles—to the Cheraws region of South Carolina, where he was told enough food could be found.

Not wishing to look like he was retreating, he bolstered General Morgan's light corps with more infantry and cavalry, and sent them in the opposite direction into South Carolina to rally the militia there.

Morgan's "Flying Camp," as it was called by General Greene, marched southwestward on December 21st. With it went John Southall and Captain Wallace's company of Virginia Continentals. After several days, they halted along the Pacolet River and waited for more militia to join them.

They also waited to see the enemy's reaction to their presence. While they waited, Christmas passed, and a few days later, John celebrated his 17th birthday. It had been an eventful year for him, but he sensed that the next, 1781, would be even more eventful. He would turn out to be right.

In Virginia, James's 18th birthday had passed by unnoticed in early December, but that was fine with him—he had always preferred to be out of the spotlight. He had been glad to return to his normal routine as a tutor, but a week before Christmas, the Nelson's surprised him by announcing a suspension of lessons until the new year.

"Go home, Mr. Southall. Go and visit your family," encouraged Mrs. Nelson.

"Or someone else in Richmond," General Nelson added with a wink.

James happily accepted the time off and rode to Williamsburg on Spartan—the same horse he'd used during the British raid two months earlier. His visit with his family was brief—just one night—for he was eager to get to Richmond and surprise Rebecca, who was expecting him to arrive on Christmas Day. He set out early in the morning and reached the Anderson's tavern late in the afternoon.

Ben, Mr. Anderson's enslaved waiter, greeted James at the door and led him to the dining room to join the Andersons.

"Mr. Southall is here, sir," Ben announced as James slid past him into the room.

Rebecca leapt to her feet and rushed toward James, then remembered herself, stopped, and curtsied.

"We didn't expect you for a week," she said, stepping closer and taking his hands.

"Spartan worked hard to get me here," James said. "He's pretty tired for the effort."

"Ben," called Mr. Anderson, "tell Will to fetch Mr. Southall's horse and put him up for the night. And make sure he gets some extra oats."

"Thank you, sir," said James with a bow to Mr. Anderson.

"Come, James! Join us at table," said Mrs. Anderson. "You must be famished after such a long ride."

"Indeed, I am, ma'am," replied James gratefully. "Thank you." James sat for dinner and answered question after question about General Nelson's family, the General himself, the recent British raid on Virginia, and his own family.

"And what have you heard from John?" Rebecca asked, eager to hear news of her friend.

"I received a letter from him about a week ago, dated mid-November. He's under the command of General Morgan somewhere near Charlotte. He thinks things have calmed down for the winter."

Rebecca folded her hands in front of her. "Let's pray he is right."

The conversation continued well after dinner, moving on to life in Richmond and the upcoming Christmas season.

"The Assembly is adjourned, so I expect a rather slow time of it," Mr. Anderson speculated. "I have no regrets about moving here—well, other than leaving Williamsburg. Which, as you know, is a far finer town than this."

James nodded in agreement, but the truth was he'd been away from Williamsburg for longer than Mr. Anderson, and had little direct knowledge of the changes that had occurred there—other than the obvious closing of the Capitol and governor's residence, and the occasional reference from his father of slow business.

"The good news," Mr. Anderson continued, "is that you get a room upstairs all to yourself."

"Thank you, sir."

"Speaking of which," declared Mrs. Anderson, rising from the table and patting her husband on the hand. "I think it is time for us to turn in."

Mr. Anderson frowned at the suggestion but rose up to comply. "Don't stay up too late," he said to Rebecca. "We still have a few guests to tend to."

"Of course, Father."

With her parents gone, James and Rebecca smiled at each other. The young couple appreciated the chance to finally be alone in the dining room.

"So, what is there to see in Richmond?" asked James. "We had our brook at home. I suppose the river will have to substitute for it."

Rebecca smiled. "It's quite the substitute. We can explore it tomorrow, if you'd like."

"That would be fine," smiled James.

They chatted on for another hour about the people who lived in Richmond and the people Rebecca had met.

Suddenly, Rebecca gave a start, her hand flying to her chest.

“Oh, I forgot to wish you a happy birthday,” she cried sadly.

“It’s fine,” James chuckled. “Just another year.”

Rebecca reached for his hand and squeezed. “What do you think the next year will have in store for us?” She didn’t dare speak of the quiet hope she held onto—that the war would end soon, that the Americans would be victorious.

James squeezed her hand back, not wanting to give voice to the quiet dread he felt, sure that the worst had yet to come. “I wish I knew,” he said quietly. “I wish I knew.”

Three hundred and fifty miles to the north in New York, General Henry Clinton had resolved that same night to send yet another British expedition to Virginia in an effort to disrupt the state’s support of the American Southern army in the Carolinas.

General Benedict Arnold, the infamous American traitor, was chosen by Clinton to lead the expedition. His arrival in Virginia before the year ended would trigger ten months of warfare in the Old Dominion, culminating in the pivotal battle of Yorktown.

James, Rebecca, their families, and the rest of Virginia would all be swept up in the conflict when the Revolutionary War returned to Virginia in 1781.

Heritage Books by Michael Cecere:

A Brave, Active, and Intrepid Soldier:
Lieutenant Colonel Richard Campbell
of the Virginia Continental Line

A Good and Valuable Officer:
Daniel Morgan in the Revolutionary War

A Universal Appearance of War:
The Revolutionary War in Virginia, 1775–1781

An Officer of Very Extraordinary Merit:
Charles Porterfield and the American War for Independence, 1775–1780

Captain Thomas Posey and the 7th Virginia Regiment

Cast Off the British Yoke:
The Old Dominion and American Independence, 1763–1776

Great Things are Expected from the Virginians:
Virginia in the American Revolution

He Fell a Cheerful Sacrifice to His Country's Glorious Cause:
General William Woodford of Virginia, Revolutionary War Patriot

In This Time of Extreme Danger:
Northern Virginia in the American Revolution

Second to No Man but the Commander in Chief:
Hugh Mercer, American Patriot

They Are Indeed a Very Useful Corps:
American Riflemen in the Revolutionary War

They Behaved Like Soldiers:
Captain John Chilton and the Third Virginia Regiment, 1775–1778

To Hazard Our Own Security:
Maine's Role in the American Revolution

Virginia's Continentals, 1775–1778: Volume One

Virginia's Continentals, 1778–1783: Volume Two

Wedded to My Sword:
The Revolutionary War Service of Light Horse Harry Lee

Williamsburg at War:
Virginia's Colonial Capital in the Revolutionary War

Witness to Revolution: Growing Up in Williamsburg During the American Revolution
Michael and Jennifer Cecere

Witness to War: The Sequel to Witness to Revolution*:*
Growing Up in Williamsburg During the American Revolution
Michael and Jennifer Cecere

www.ingramcontent.com/pod-product-compliance
Lightning Source LLC
LaVergne TN
LVHW050613100826
845148LV00011B/1565